Cody ran over to Olivia's window and stared at it.

"He's alerting," Henry declared. "The explosive is attached to your apartment window. We have to get out of here!"

Grabbing her cat, Olivia ignored its howling protest and ran with Henry and Cody. They'd only made it a few steps down the hall when Henry's cell phone dinged, stopping them both in their tracks. Dread gripped Olivia as she pressed close to Henry to read the incoming text.

Ka-BOOM!

TRUE BLUE K-9 UNIT: BROOKLYN

These police officers fight for justice with the help of their brave canine partners.

Terri Reed's romance and romantic suspense novels have appeared on the *Publishers Weekly* top twenty-five and Nielsen BookScan top one hundred lists, and have been featured in *USA TODAY*, *Christian Fiction* magazine and *RT Book Reviews*. Her books have been finalists for the Romance Writers of America RITA® Award and the National Readers' Choice Award, and finalists three times for the American Christian Fiction Writers Carol Award. Contact Terri at terrireed.com or PO Box 19555, Portland, OR 97224.

Books by Terri Reed

Love Inspired Suspense

Buried Mountain Secrets
Secret Mountain Hideout

True Blue K-9 Unit: Brooklyn

Explosive Situation

True Blue K-9 Unit

Seeking the Truth

Military K-9 Unit

Tracking Danger
Mission to Protect

Visit the Author Profile page at Harlequin.com for more titles.

EXPLOSIVE
SITUATION
TERRI REED

LOVE INSPIRED SUSPENSE
INSPIRATIONAL ROMANCE

Special thanks and acknowledgment
are given to Terri Reed for her contribution
to the True Blue K-9 Unit: Brooklyn miniseries.

LOVE INSPIRED®SUSPENSE
INSPIRATIONAL ROMANCE

ISBN-13: 978-1-335-57454-1

Explosive Situation

Love Inspired
22 Adelaide St. West, 40th Floor
Toronto, Ontario M5H 4E3, Canada
www.Harlequin.com

Printed in U.S.A.

Recycling programs
for this product may
not exist in your area.

Trust in the Lord with all thine heart;
and lean not unto thine own understanding. In all thy ways
acknowledge him, and he shall direct thy paths.
–*Proverbs* 3:5-6

Thank you to my family for all the support and love.

ONE

A prickle of unease tingled at the base of K-9 detective Henry Roarke's neck. Squirreled away in the records room of the recently formed Brooklyn K-9 unit with his bomb-sniffing beagle, Cody, lying at his feet and dozens of his fellow officers in the building, he knew there was no reason for the unsettling sensation of being watched. Yet it was something that he had been feeling the past several months. Even before the incident that had landed him in hot water.

Eyeing Cody, who lifted his head but made no sound, Henry couldn't decide if he was being paranoid or had just been cooped up in here too long, especially with the humid July heat adding its own special brand of oppression to the windowless room. Yet he couldn't shake the disquiet alerting his senses.

With slow, deliberate movements, he set down the file folder he held, straightened his spine and turned around, fully expecting to find an empty doorway. Instead, his gaze collided with the amber-colored eyes of Internal Affairs Lieutenant Olivia Vance. He suppressed a groan of frustration.

She stood tall and regal in a black pantsuit with her brunette hair pulled back into some sort of fancy bun, which emphasized the slender column of her neck visible above the collar of her white shirt. Her tawny skin had the glow of health and her full lips were tinged a slightly rosy color that emphasized her very feminine and pretty mouth. He jerked his gaze back to her eyes.

The woman exuded a professional aptitude that would normally draw Henry in. He liked women who were confident and sure of their place in the world—not that he'd dated much the past six years. After his long-term girlfriend Kathy's refusal to bond with Riley, he'd made a vow not to let anyone in his life until his sister was on her own.

Except this woman was here to dig into his life, not start a romance. Olivia was tasked with determining whether the allegations brought against him by a twenty-something-year-old punk, who'd resisted arrest and made a grab for his sidearm, were reason enough to recommend to the review board that Henry be brought up on assault charges. Charges that would end a career he loved.

Sharply turning back to the mound of folders he was organizing, Henry asked, "Can I help you, Lieutenant?"

"I need to interview you."

He slanted a glance at her.

"If you would please accompany me to an interrogation room." She gestured to the open doorway and empty hall behind her.

Jaw clenching, Henry marshaled his irritation as best he could. "With all due respect, ma'am, I've already spoken to Lieutenant Jabboski. Can't you read his report?"

Olivia's delicately dark, winged eyebrows

rose. "I'm sorry to inform you that Lieutenant Jabboski's skills as an investigator were lacking. He made few notes and relied heavily on his gut feelings. I, however, do not."

The original Internal Affairs investigator had recently suffered a mild heart attack and retired, leaving the investigation to be completed by the recently promoted Olivia. Though Henry had never met the woman, he'd known of her for years. He was friends with her two older brothers, both officers working out of Manhattan precincts and also knew one of her sisters, a paramedic. Each had described Olivia as a taskmaster, meticulous and overbearing. Traits that lent themselves to the career she'd chosen.

"Because I am basically starting from the beginning," the lieutenant continued, "I need to hear from you regarding the events that took place on the night in question."

Henry's coworkers had already been interviewed by the Internal Affairs lieutenant. And no matter how much each one had assured him that the investigation wouldn't amount to anything, anxiety twisted in his chest. Now it was his turn to fall under this woman's scrutiny. "I'd like my union rep to be present."

After a second's hesitation, she inclined her head. "That is your right. I will wait to hear from you and set up a time in the future. Meanwhile, have fun with your file folders—though I seriously doubt any of them are about to explode."

Henry drew back his chin at the jab. "Excuse me?"

She shrugged and gave him a smile that didn't reach her eyes. "I was told you were chomping at the bit to get back to full duty. Apparently, I was misinformed." She turned to go.

"Lieutenant, wait!" Henry was indeed eager to reclaim his position on the bomb squad. He was tired of the menial assignments and there was only so much training he and Cody could do in a day before the dog needed a break. "I've changed my mind. We can do this now. Here."

He'd talk to her without his union rep because he hadn't done anything wrong, but he wasn't about to let her put him in an interrogation room like he was some criminal suspect.

For a moment, she seemed to consider his words, then nodded before withdrawing a small notepad and pen from her suit jacket. She stepped just inside the doorway. "Okay, then. Tell me about the night of March twenty-seventh."

Resigning himself to repeating what he'd told Jabboski, Henry said, "A call came in about a possible bomb threat at Owl's Head Park's skate park. When we—"

The chime of an incoming text on his cell phone filled the room. Henry grabbed the device from the top of the filing cabinet. He hoped the text was from his sister saying she had made it safely home from her summer class at Brooklyn College.

He still wasn't used to the idea of his baby sister going to college. She'd elected to take summer classes to jump-start her freshmen year. Plus, it would keep her busy because her regular summer job of nanny for the neighbors was on hold while the family was out west visiting relatives.

"Excuse me," Olivia's voice snapped. "We're in the middle of an interview."

Henry met her gaze. "I understand, ma'am. This will only take a minute."

He opened his text messages, aware of Olivia's displeasure emanating from her like daggers poking into his skin. He turned his back while he read the text. It was from Riley. She was on her way to Coney Island. Her class had ended over an hour ago. No doubt she was already at the boardwalk and texting him had been an afterthought. She was in so much trouble.

He blew out a breath as he quickly typed a response, reminding her they'd discussed her going straight home after her class. She may be eighteen and technically an adult, but until she was on her own and not living under his roof, she still had to abide by his rules. And she'd just broken one.

He pinched the bridge of his nose as he set the phone back on the filing cabinet. His head throbbed with a brewing headache.

Why had no one told him parenting a teenager would be so difficult? He didn't regret taking in his half sibling after the death of their father and her mother six years ago. But there were times when he pondered what it would be like to be free of this constant gnawing worry.

"Can we proceed?" Olivia's voice was edged in impatience.

"Yes, ma'am." He couldn't believe he had to go through this again. He had had complete confidence that Lieutenant Jabboski would have told the review board that Henry had acted appropriately. Now the investigation was starting from scratch. And with the disapproving glare that this woman was serving him, he doubted she would find much in his favor.

Reining in his frustration, he said, "When Cody and I, along with Detective Bradley McGregor and his K-9, arrived—"

His phone chimed again with another incoming text. He cringed. Now what? He hoped Riley was saying she was headed home.

Olivia cleared her throat. "Can you please put away your phone and set it to silent?"

"Sorry. It's my sister, Riley." He snatched up the phone.

Family came first for him, always.

Only this wasn't from Riley. The incoming text came from a number he didn't recognize. His mouth dried as he read the words.

Knock knock. Who's there? Joey Yums. Joey Yums who? Joey Yums goes kaboooom—at 3:20 LOLZ

Henry's stomach dropped. Joey Yums was a hole-in-the-wall falafel joint at the far end of the Coney Island boardwalk and one of his sister's favorite places to eat when they visited the area.

He checked the time on his phone and panic exploded in his chest, making his body shake. It would take twenty to thirty minutes to reach the restaurant from the station, depending on traffic—barely time to arrive and remove people from the vicinity, let alone disarm an explosive device. But he had to try. Riley was in danger. His veins flooded with adrenaline. He quickly sent her a text warning her to stay away from Joey Yums and go home. Now. He grabbed Cody's leash. "Time to work."

He pushed past Olivia and hurried out of the records room in search of his sergeant.

"Excuse me!" Olivia's voice rang out with indignation. "We're not done here. And you aren't allowed to work."

"I have to go. Lives are in danger." He went straight to the front desk, leaving Olivia staring after him, her gaze like a heavy weight on his shoulders.

"I need Gavin now," he told Penny McGregor, his friend and colleague, and Bradley's younger sister.

"He's out on a call," she told him. "But I can contact him."

Having no other choice, Henry had to make sure his sister and everyone else was safe. "You do that. Tell him Joey Yums restaurant in Coney Island. A bomb threat.

We're on it. Alert the sixtieth precinct to meet us in front of Joey Yums."

Without waiting for a reply, he headed out the door as his fingers flew across his text message screen, writing to his boss. He had to let Gavin know what he was doing. Henry had no doubt he'd end up in hot water, but at the moment, he didn't care. Riley was his only family and innocent lives were at stake.

He reached his vehicle, a large white SUV with blue lettering identifying the K-9 unit. The back passenger area was outfitted with a large compartment for Cody and a smaller passenger space for suspect transportation. Behind that was cargo space for his and Cody's equipment.

A question ricocheted through his mind: How had this bomber managed to get a hold of his personal cell phone number?

A good dose of irritation, annoyance and stunned outrage engulfed Olivia as she raced to keep up with the towering, fast-moving officer while stuffing her notebook and pen back into her suit pocket.

The summer sun glistened off his shaved head and deepened the bronze angles of his handsome face. He presented a formidable adversary with a well-toned, muscular body beneath his dark blue uniform. His shoulders were wide and his bearing that of someone who was used to being in control.

Which irked her to no end.

Her late husband had wanted to control her and that had caused issues in their marriage, which left her with a bitter taste in her mouth. She was done with controlling men.

Olivia caught up to him at his vehicle. "Where do you think you're going? You're on modified duty. Which means you are not to leave the station."

He opened the back passenger door and lifted Cody into the K-9 unit's caged compartment.

The moment he shut the door, Olivia planted herself in front of the driver-side door. The intensity in his dark eyes was both daunting and frightening, but she had two older brothers who had mastered the art of intimidation. Henry's ire didn't faze her. She blew out a breath. "Your refusal to obey orders doesn't bode well for you."

"With all due respect, this investigation is a sham. The kid is lying. I didn't hurt him. And I know how to follow orders. I'm former Army."

She'd read in his file that he'd served. Combat soldier with a medal of valor. Impressive, but she couldn't let that sway her. "Then you should stay put and let someone else deal with the situation."

"I can't." He reached past her, his hand grabbing the door handle. He was taller than her by at least four inches, which was a lot considering she was almost six feet tall. His arm brushed against her shoulder, the friction disconcerting.

"Why? Where are you going?"

"Coney Island," he said sharply. "That second text was a bomb threat."

Her stomach contracted with a wave of anxiety. A bomb? "There's a bomb hidden somewhere on the Coney Island beach or boardwalk?"

"Yes." He faced her. His dark eyes filled with worry. "I don't care if you take my job away. My sister is there, and she's in danger. I'm going. As a police officer or not. Time is of the essence. Come with me or not, the choice is yours."

Stunned by that bit of news, Olivia understood now why he was so anxious to get to Coney Island. And his sister was involved. She understood family loyalty.

Her two brothers would react the same way, not caring that they were risking their lives or their careers, if one of their three sisters needed them. Apparently, Henry was the same. Grudging respect filled her and she mentally tucked away the knowledge.

Without another word, she ran around the front of his vehicle, keeping her hand on the hood to make sure he didn't leave without her as he jumped in and started the engine.

She quickly climbed into the passenger seat. She'd barely shut the door before he peeled out of the parking lot behind the K-9 unit building with sirens blaring. Even with her seat belt fastened, she had to hang on with both hands to keep from being thrown about the inside of the cab as he drove out of the Bay Ridge neighborhood like a man on a mission. Which she supposed he was.

Everything about this man was sharp. Sharp edges, sharp tongue and sharp anger. She'd done her research before confronting him today. His fellow K-9 officers spoke highly of him. All trusting his judgment. His superior had said Henry was top notch. One of the best.

Even his instructors at the police academy praised him and his dog.

But the man sitting beside her didn't appear to be a man in control. More like a man desperate to protect someone he loved. What had happened the night of Davey Carrell's injuries? Had Henry lost his cool as Davey claimed, bending Davey's wrist to the point of breaking and elbowing the kid in the neck, causing strain to the muscles there?

She had to admit Henry drove with skill

and focus. Even at this breakneck speed, she felt safe. For both herself and the child growing inside of her.

His phone blew up with incoming text messages. He ignored them and concentrated on the road. She had to admire his commitment to no texting and driving. "Should I read your text messages?"

He sped through an intersection. "Yes. Please."

She plucked his phone from the pocket of his shirt where she'd seen him drop it. Leaning close to him, she got a whiff of his spicy aftershave that momentarily stalled her hand. The scent was something she'd never smelled before. Unusual and very masculine. Giving herself a shake, she looked at the lock screen, thankful he didn't have a privacy setting. The texts were all from his boss, Sergeant Gavin Sutherland.

Swiping up, she was able to read the furious missives from his boss. "Your sergeant says he's dispatched a local bomb squad and will meet you there."

She studied Henry's profile. His jaw was

clenched so tightly she was surprised she didn't hear his teeth cracking. He didn't bother to glance away from the road, but gave a sharp nod of his head. "I need you to text my sister again. Tell her to leave now if she hasn't already and meet us at the corner of West 12th and Bowery. And to stay away from Joey Yums."

She scrolled through his text contacts until she found his sister Riley's name. She read the last two texts. The one that had come in at the beginning of the interview and the one he sent back, reprimanding her for not going straight home after her classes, the tone more fatherly than brotherly.

Considering he'd raised his sister alone for the past six years, she wasn't too surprised, but somehow the idea of this man as a father tugged at her in unexpected ways. Giving herself another mental shake, she quickly sent a text to Riley giving her the information.

No answering text came in. Olivia stared at the device as if she could will the teenager to respond. She sent up a silent plea heavenward for God to prompt Riley to look at her phone. Was this what parenthood would be like? Worrying, waiting and praying?

She needed to talk to her brothers' wives and ask how they coped with motherhood.

Henry brought the vehicle to a screeching halt at an angle at the curb of West 12th and Bowery. The iconic state park was bursting with activity along the famous boardwalk, the amusement park rides were filled with tourists and locals alike, and the sandy beaches sported sunbathers on blankets or children and adults frolicking in the waves.

He jumped out and slammed the door. Quickly, she followed suit. By the time she made it around to his side of the vehicle, he had Cody already leashed up and was talking to him in a quiet, soft voice. She wouldn't have deemed him capable of such tenderness, especially in the midst of a bomb threat. Another aspect of him to tuck away for further analysis.

She handed Henry back his phone. "She hasn't replied." His distress ratcheted up her own nervousness. "She probably put her phone in her purse and can't hear it." She hoped that was the case.

Henry tucked the phone in his pocket.

"Where to now?" she asked.

"Joey Yums."

She had no idea where that was, or even what it was, for that matter. "I'm coming with you."

If she stuck close to him, she could observe and record his behavior for her report. Seeing him and his dog in action would help her to better form an opinion of his work habits and ethics.

He hesitated, concern etched on his handsome face, then he said, "Let's go." He and Cody took off at a run.

She hurried after them, glad she'd worn her flats today with her suit. She couldn't imagine running on the planked boardwalk in heels. Huffing with the speed at which she ran to keep up with Henry and Cody, she was thankful when the pair slowed outside of a restaurant.

Two police officers from the local precinct stood nearby. From the fresh face of the younger officer, Olivia guessed him to be a rookie. Protocol was for the first on scene to wait for the supervising agency, in this case the Brooklyn K-9 Unit, to arrive before starting evacuation, because opening doors without having them checked by explosive experts could result in disaster.

Henry halted at the older officer's side. "Set a perimeter while we evacuate the restaurant." Henry pointed to the eating establishment then glanced at his watch. "According to the text message we have seven minutes before detonation. We have to clear the place."

Olivia's lungs squeezed tight. "You can't go in there, Henry."

Had she just called him Henry instead of Detective? The texts from his sister, his worry, the imminent danger made this suddenly more...personal.

He stared at her for a heartbeat. "May I call you Olivia?"

She lifted her chin and then nodded.

"Olivia, we're trained for this. Waiting will result in destruction."

He was right. Civilian lives were at stake. "Go." She prayed she was making the right decision.

Henry and Cody hurried forward. Cody sniffed around the entrance without alerting before they disappeared inside.

Staring after them, worry wormed through her. Within moments, a stream of people rushed out of the restaurant. She and the two officers hustled the crowd away. She was thankful to have something useful to do while Henry and Cody searched for the bomb. And she was just as thankful the smells of Coney Island weren't causing her stomach to rebel. She was glad to be done with the morning sickness that had plagued her the first trimester of her pregnancy.

More officers arrived. A man in a full explosive ordnance disposal suit headed for the entrance to the restaurant. She quickly ascertained the officer in charge and explained that Henry and Cody had already gone inside. Officers set up a barrier around the restaurant, asking people to vacate the area.

Not knowing what else to do, Olivia joined

in. "Please back up. You need to leave the boardwalk."

Many people moved back but several remained to watch, and some scurried off. Her gaze scanned the growing crowd of onlookers. Was the bomber among the gawkers?

Henry's boss and his partner arrived on scene. Olivia recognized Sergeant Gavin Sutherland and his dog, Tommy, a brown and white springer spaniel. She rushed to him and brought him up to speed on what was happening.

"He did the right thing, you know," Gavin said.

She nodded. Even though he'd disobeyed orders, she couldn't fault him for putting the safety of others ahead of his own interests. Something her late husband would never have thought of, let alone done.

A moment later, Cody and Henry walked out. Henry held up his hands in a gesture of confusion and shaking his head. "Nothing. Cody didn't alert on anything."

"We'll take it from here," Gavin said.

"You cooperate with Lieutenant Vance. We need you back on duty!"

"Yes, sir," Henry replied, though his troubled gaze scanned their surroundings.

Gavin and Tommy walked back toward the restaurant.

"Has your sister responded?" Olivia asked.

His anxiety obvious in the tightness around his mouth and the concern in his eyes, he shook his head. "Do you mind if we search for her?"

Deciding neither of them would be able to concentrate until they were sure his sister was safe, she nodded. "Let's find Riley."

Figuring Riley had headed for Luna Park, Henry and Cody led Olivia at a fast clip toward the amusement park rides. He kept an eye out for any sign of Riley among the throng of summertime visitors. His phone chimed. Finally. He read the message and his stomach dropped. Same phone number as before. His steps faltered as the words on the phone's screen registered like a loud clanging in his ears.

Oh, did I say Joey Yums? I meant the garbage can. Kaboom! LOLZ

A fresh wave of panic hit Henry. There
were several trash bins on the boardwalk
and inside the park. "Cody, seek!"

"What's going on?" Olivia asked.

"Another bomb threat," he told her as he
and Cody hustled toward the nearest garbage can. Nose working the ground and
the air, the beagle moved past the round
metal containers. Then he let out a loud bark
and strained against his leash. Clearly he'd
picked up a scent.

Running to keep up, Henry let Cody lead
him down the boardwalk. Cody's feet scrab-
bled on the wooden planks as he neared a
garbage can that had been moved from the
center aisle and placed beside a bench where
a young couple sat kissing.

The dog halted in front of the trash can
and stared at it. His signal that he'd found
an explosive.

Fearing for his dog, Henry gave a sharp
whistle, Cody's signal to return. The dog

immediately responded. Running toward the couple, Henry waved his arms and shouted, "Off the bench! Run. Now!"

The garbage can exploded.

TWO

Muted screams penetrated the ringing in Olivia's ears. Crouched, she protected her head with her hands. All around, people were taking cover. Trash and sand rained down, stinging her back and hands.

Peeking around her elbows, she watched Henry, a few feet away, scoop up his dog and cradle Cody in his arms. Henry's back had taken the force of the blast. The young couple who had been sitting on the bench beside the garbage can had heard Henry's warning and were halfway over the railing separating the boardwalk from the beach when the bomb detonated. Now both were lying in the sand.

The world settled into a stunned silence as the echo of the explosion dissipated. Olivia cautiously rose, assessing any injuries to her person and deemed herself unharmed. The baby moved, the slight sensation reassuring. She rushed forward. "Detective Roarke? Are you hurt?"

Henry set Cody on the ground then straightened and faced her. His dark eyes blazed with anger and concern. "I'm good. You?"

"Fine." Though her heart raced at a fast clip.

On the beach, the couple sat up and appeared to have minor injuries. Henry headed toward the spot where half of the bench had been ripped away and a charred circle remained on the ground where the garbage can had once stood. Now the can rested on its side a few feet away. There was a ragged hole where the explosive device had ripped through the metal.

"That could have been my sister," Henry's horrified whisper tugged at Olivia. "I have to find her."

"It seems a bit too coincidental that the bomber would contact you at the same time your sister is in the vicinity," Olivia stated aloud. She hadn't put the two together until now. Were the Roarkes being targeted?

Pressing a hand over her abdomen where the small round bump pressed against her clothing, protective instincts surged through her so strongly she shivered.

The thought of something happening to the child growing inside of her... Nausea, different from her previous bout of morning sickness, rolled in her stomach. She lifted a silent prayer to God for protection and glanced up to find Henry's intent gaze locked on her like a laser. She dropped her hand away. At his raised eyebrow, heat infused her cheeks. The man noticed way too much. The last thing she needed was for him to realize she was pregnant. She didn't want anyone treating her differently because of the baby.

Finding her voice, Olivia said, "How do we find your sister?"

His eyebrows dipped and for a moment she was afraid he was going to ask questions that she'd rather not answer. Then he pulled his phone out of his shirt pocket and typed in a text.

Sirens punctuated the air. The officers who'd converged on Joey Yums now flooded the boardwalk, quick to preserve the area for the crime scene investigators.

An ambulance rolled to a stop nearby and two paramedics jumped out. Olivia met the surprised gaze of her youngest sister, Ally.

After saying something to her partner, Ally grabbed a big red box and jogged to Olivia's side. "What happened? Are you okay? The baby?"

"Shhhh," Olivia hissed and shot a quick glance at Henry to see if he'd heard. His gaze was trained on the crowd that had gathered to watch. She prayed he hadn't been paying attention to her sister's questions.

Ally was shining a penlight into Olivia's eyes. "What?"

Batting her sister away, she said, "I'm fine, Ally. It's those two I'm worried about." She pointed to the two young people sitting on the sand, now flanked by officers.

"Jake, we've got two injured on the beach,"

Ally called out to her partner, who nodded and headed in that direction.

Ally turned her brown gaze to Henry. "Whoa, Henry, you have a cut on your head." She opened her box and pulled out gauze and tape.

Olivia wasn't surprised that Ally and Henry were familiar with each other. Despite the size of the Brooklyn borough, first responders and law enforcement were a tight-knit community. Except when it came to Internal Affairs.

She'd experienced firsthand the cool disdain most everyone in uniform held for the division that investigated its own. It was uncomfortable, at best, and downright disturbing most of time. Not to mention lonely and isolating. And no matter how much she tried not to let the drawbacks to the job get to her, there were days she regretted the professional track she'd chosen.

Henry put his hand to the back of his head and pulled it away to reveal dark red blood smeared on his palm.

Olivia sucked in a breath. "You *are* hurt."

He gave a negative shake of his head. "I barely feel the wound."

Stubborn man. Of course he wouldn't admit to any pain. That would be too much like admitting to being human.

"Well, I need you to sit so I can bandage your laceration," Ally told him.

Olivia pointed to the nearest bench. "Sit."

Henry's startled gaze met hers. "Yes, ma'am."

Henry took a seat so Ally could dress his wound.

"You should make an appointment with your primary doctor to make sure there's no concussion," Ally said as she finished up.

"I will," he promised. "But I have something I need to do first."

Olivia put her hand on his shoulder, keeping him from rising. "Take a breath."

Ally rose, gathered her things and said to Olivia, "I'll let you tell Mom and Dad about this."

Olivia grimaced. "Thanks. Honestly, they don't need to know."

"You really think Dad won't hear about

this incident?" Ally shook her head, her golden-brown ponytail swishing. "I better go help Jake." Taking her red supply kit with her, she hurried away.

Olivia glanced at Henry, who stared at his phone as if willing it to ding. Cody sat at his feet, waiting patiently for his next job.

Her sister was right. Their father, a captain with the NYPD, would learn that his oldest daughter was at the scene of a bombing. Not a usual day in Internal Affairs. She'd worked hard to make the rank of lieutenant and hoped to make her parents proud. But after the death of her husband, her life had spun out of her control. She wasn't quite sure how to handle the grief, the betrayal, the anger. Most days it was easiest to pretend she didn't feel anything at all.

Henry stood, bracing his legs apart for a moment as if to steady himself.

Concern arced through Olivia. She put a hand out to help him then thought better of it, letting her hand drop back to her side. She empathized with his worry and could only imagine the strike to his head hurt, but giving into her natural inclination to support and comfort wouldn't serve her position as an Internal Affairs investigator well. And that really was a source of irritation that she needed to suppress.

"Henry." Sergeant Gavin Sutherland jogged to their side.

Henry squared his shoulders and faced his boss. "Sarge."

"Lieutenant," Gavin greeted with a nod.

She returned the gesture of respect.

Eyes narrowed on the white bandage on Henry's scalp, Gavin said, "After you write up the incident report, take the rest of the day off. Visit a doctor. I don't want you back at the station until Monday."

"Yes, sir," Henry said. "I have to collect my sister and then I'll stop by the precinct to write up my report. Can you give Lieutenant Vance a ride, sir?"

Olivia gaped at Henry, pretty sure she looked like a fish landing on the dock of her family's vacation spot. He was trying to get rid of her. Not so fast. "That won't be necessary. I'll go with you to find your sister. You took a nasty blow to the head. I wouldn't want you to collapse on the board-walk."

"I'm not—" he protested but she held up a hand.

"I insist." She smiled sweetly to soften her words. She outranked both of these men. "I still need to interview you."

A frown pulled his dark eyebrows to-gether. "I'm sorry, can't that wait?"

"No. Why else do you think I came with you?"

Gavin stared at her a moment before say-ing, "Do as the Lieutenant wishes, Henry. Someone has to be there in case that hard head of yours decides to explode."

"Har, har, Sarge," Henry muttered, tossing his boss a small smile. All the K-9 officers at the Brooklyn K-9 Unit had grown close in a short time, and a little ribbing on one an-other, even from Sarge, always helped with tension. He turned to Olivia and said, "By all means," then addressed his dog. "Let's find Riley."

Cody gave a sharp yelp as if in agreement.

Olivia nodded to the sergeant, then fell into step with Henry. "You and Cody were very brave back there."

"We were doing our job," he said. "Which we're good at, by the way."

"I know you find this process arduous but it's necessary," she said. "Allegations of police brutality must be taken seriously."

His jaw firmed but he made no comment as his stride lengthened. The beagle had no trouble staying in step with his handler and it was obvious Cody's nose was working, sniffing through the various odors permeating the air. She had to move quicker to keep up.

They entered the Luna Park amusement area filled with rides for all ages, a variety of foods, games to play and shopping. All around them, people had gone back to their fun as if the exploding garbage can on the nearby boardwalk hadn't happened. She didn't understand it. "Don't any of these people realize how close they came to disaster?"

Henry glanced at her, then away. "In my

experience, most people view danger as something that happens to others. As long as it doesn't interfere with their own lives, they ignore what could harm them. Besides, considering last week was the 4th of July, most of these people probably figured the noise was leftover fireworks."

She supposed he was correct. Still, the danger had been real. Once again, the protective instinct to cover the child inside of her with a comforting hand on her abdomen flooded her veins, but she refrained.

Henry placed his hand to the small of her back and guided her around a line waiting for the roller coaster. Cody sniffed each person he passed. Henry's gaze scanned the crowd. She was glad he wasn't looking at her because she was sure her expression would give away her shock at his touch.

"Finally. There's Riley."

Following the line of his gaze to a pretty young woman with dark ringlets and a wide smile standing near the front of the line of the roller coaster with some friends, Coney Island Cyclone, Olivia smiled. The resemblance to Henry was unmistakable. They shared the same deep bronze skin, dark wide eyes and high cheekbones. Both were tall, though Riley still had the gangly look of a teen while Henry was all muscle and strength.

If Henry pulled Riley out of line now, the teenager would be both embarrassed and angry. Olivia turned to Henry. "Let her have her ride."

Doubt clouded his eyes but then he sighed and nodded. After having Cody sniff the perimeter of the ride and those standing in line and seeing no sign of alert, Henry and Olivia moved to the shade of a tree to wait for his sister to come off the roller coaster. Cody sat at Henry's feet as if waiting for his next command.

Seizing on the opportunity, she took her notebook out of her pocket and, with pen poised, said, "You were telling me about the night at Owl's Head Park."

Henry folded his arms over his chest, his gaze scanning the area as he spoke. "Cody alerted to a backpack sitting off to one side.

The owner of the backpack tried to take the bag and leave. We detained him and he resisted. Then he made a grab for my sidearm."

She scribbled as he talked. Glancing up from her notes, she said, "That is the point when Mr. Carrell sustained his injuries?"

"Allegedly," Henry bit out. "I didn't break that kid's wrist."

"Then can you explain how the injury happened?"

He shook his head. "I have no idea. If I was going to break something on the suspect I would have gone for his elbow. But I didn't."

A shudder at the image his words evoked rippled through her. Eying his muscular arms, she had no doubt he could snap a bone.

"He also sustained an injury to his neck," she commented, forcing herself back on track. "I suppose you didn't do that, either?"

His gaze flicked to her, hard and unyielding. "Olivia, I used a defensive tactic to prevent the suspect from relieving me of my duty weapon."

"And Detective McGregor witnessed this altercation?"

The muscles in Henry's neck tightened. "Bradley was managing the crowd."

"Right. So he didn't actually see Mr. Carrell grab for your weapon."

"No. If Bradley had been able to corroborate my story, none of this would be happening."

That was true. And unfortunate for Henry that Bradley McGregor hadn't witnessed the altercation. "How did you secure your weapon?"

"The way I was trained," he replied. "I grabbed his right hand, which held my weapon, while wedging my other forearm into the curve of his neck and pushing him backward until he released his hold on my sidearm. Would you like me to show you?"

She blinked, intrigued by the offer. Would a demonstration of this tactic support Henry's version of the story? "Maybe that would be a good idea."

His head jerked back and he stared at her. "Really?"

She suppressed a smile at his surprise. "Yes, really. But we will have to table that for another day. For now, we'll stick with questions. You didn't find an explosive device in the backpack, correct?"

He heaved a beleaguered sigh. "No, we did not."

"But Cody alerted?" She'd witnessed the dog in action today. Both the dog and handler were competent. They worked well together. She could understand why his sergeant wanted him back on duty.

"He did."

"A false alert?"

"No way. The NYPD's forensic specialist found nonvisible trace amounts of particulates on the bag."

"But you did not find a bomb."

"No. However, that doesn't mean there wasn't some sort of incendiary device inside the bag at one time. The department searched the residence of his parents where he said he was living. His parents seemed confused, but they corroborated that he was their son and that he had a room at their home." He let out a scoff. "At least that was the report I heard from my coworkers. Since I was not allowed to question anyone or investigate the case."

His frustration was palpable but couldn't be helped. "Had you ever had a run-in with Mr. Carrell prior to this?"

"No, I had not."

"Has Cody ever given you a false alert?"

The dog's ears perked up as if he, too, waited to hear the answer.

Henry clenched his teeth together. "One time. During training."

"Ah. He has a record of giving a false alert." Surprising after what she'd seen today, but she made a note.

"Only the one time during training in the early days."

His sharp tone had her lifting her eyebrows.

He dipped his chin, as if checking his attitude. "Sorry, Olivia."

Abruptly, Henry shifted, taking a protective stance in front of her as his gaze swiveled and he slowly turned in all directions as if expecting a threat. Cody seemed to read his master's mood because the beagle stood, his nose in the air.

Henry's sudden anxiety caused a cascade of alarm to flush through Olivia. She placed her hand on her sidearm hidden beneath her suit jacket. "What's wrong?"

"I don't know." His words came out measured, as if he were barely breathing.

"Something has you spooked." She glanced around. Was the bomber here? Would another text come in telling them an additional bomb had been planted in the vicinity or somewhere else?

After several tense seconds, he grimaced. "Paranoia."

"Or a cop's instincts." Olivia kept her own gaze vigilant.

He gestured to where Riley and her friends were exiting the roller coaster ride. "Here we go."

They approached the trio of teens.

"Henry? What are you doing here?" Riley gasped. "What happened to your head?"

"We need to leave," he barked.

Riley pulled a face. "Why?"

"I've been texting you," he said.

"My phone's in my bag. I haven't checked it lately. What's going on?" Riley's gaze bounced to Olivia and back to her brother.

Henry told the girls about the bomb on the boardwalk. "For whatever reason, this bomber has decided to communicate with me. I would rather you were home safe so I don't have to worry."

"Henry," the young woman's voice rose with pleading. She glanced at her friends, clearly embarrassed by being brought to heel by her older sibling, yet there was no mistaking the concern in her dark eyes.

Olivia could appreciate the conflicting emotions warring through the young woman. Being the eldest girl, many times the responsibility for her siblings landed on Olivia's shoulders. A point of contention with her brothers and sisters. Moved by the need to diffuse the situation, Olivia stepped forward and extended her hand. "Hi Riley, I'm Olivia."

The girl blinked then took her hand. "Olivia? Aren't you the Internal Affairs officer investigating my brother?"

"I am," she confirmed, sliding a glance at Henry. Obviously, he had talked about her. Probably disparagingly.

That was the way of it for most IA personnel. The rank and file weren't fond of those who chose to police the police. And though she fought to not let the wariness and resentment directed toward Internal Affairs affect her, it did. The solitary nature of the job was beginning to grate on her nerves.

Stifling a sigh, she said, "I was with your brother when he received the threatening text. He was very concerned about you being in the vicinity of the bomb."

Riley's gaze darted to Henry and back to Olivia. Realization shined bright in the young woman's dark eyes. "Were you hurt because of me?"

Shaking his head, Henry was quick to say, "No. This is not on you."

Riley turned to her friends. "I'll catch you all later."

"You both should go home, as well," Henry interjected. "If I had my way, the whole park would be shut down."

Riley's two friends exchanged a glance then said in unison, "Yes, sir."

Henry nodded. "We'll walk you to the subway."

Riley turned to him eagerly. "Can I go home with them?"

He shook his head. "No. You'll come with me."

Disappointment flared in her eyes, but she didn't argue. "Fine. But I'll walk with my friends."

After making sure Riley's friends were safely on their way home on the subway, Henry hustled Olivia, Riley and Cody back to his vehicle where he secured Cody in his specially designed compartment and gave him some water.

"I can take the back seat," Olivia said to Riley.

The girl shook her head. "Naw. It's fine."

Riley sat in the space reserved for suspect transport and slumped down in the seat, putting her head back and closing her eyes.

Shrugging, Olivia climbed in front. "We should head to your doctor's office."

Starting the engine, Henry replied, "They're closed by now."

"You heard my sister," she reminded him.

"I'll follow up with the doc tomorrow," he said.

Needing the reassurance that he would, she asked, "Do you promise?"

He met her gaze, confusion lighting the dark depths of his eyes. "Sure."

Hoping he was a man of his word, she settled in. He no doubt wondered why she cared enough to elicit the promise. If they were truly colleagues instead of adversaries, would he be confused by her concern? Not likely. It aggravated her to no end that everyone in the police bureau treated her and the other IA officers as the enemy in every situation.

All she'd ever wanted to do was help. But she'd allowed herself to get caught up in the need to achieve and make her family proud. There were days she wasn't sure the status was worth it.

The ride back to Bay Ridge was quiet inside the SUV. Henry brought the vehicle to a halt in front of the K-9 Unit headquarters, an attractive limestone, three-story building that once housed a police precinct that had outgrown the space.

Hunger pains gripped Olivia's stomach in an audible symphony. Embarrassment heated her face.

"Hey, anyone want to grab a pizza?" Riley gestured toward Sal's Pizzeria two doors down from the K-9 Unit.

"I shouldn't." Though Olivia's mouth watered at the thought of gooey cheese, pepperoni and veggies.

Riley hopped out of the vehicle. "Why not? You have to eat, right? And I'm starving."

"I can wait until I get home," Olivia offered. Her stomach rumbled once again, denying her claim.

Henry's mouth tipped up at the corners.

"I'd appreciate it if you'd accompany Riley. I have to write a report and feed Cody. I really don't want her to be alone."

The congenial tone of his voice wrapped around Olivia. The baby inside of her wiggled as if affected by him, as well. Henry trusted her with his sister. She couldn't deny the pleasant sensation sliding over her limbs. Telling herself it wouldn't be a bad thing to get to know Riley and gain some more insight into Henry, Olivia threaded her arm around Riley's. "I could eat a whole pizza by myself."

"Me, too," Riley said with a laugh.

Henry waited until Olivia and Riley entered the local pizza joint, known for being a favorite with the police officers in the area. Established by a retired officer and his wife long before the K-9 Unit landed nearby, Sal's was as safe as the precinct as far as Henry was concerned. The men and women in blue would keep an eye on his baby sister. Though he questioned how Olivia would fare. IA officers were rarely popular.

He turned to go inside when the hair at the base of his neck prickled with apprehension. He glanced around, searching for the threat. No one seemed overly interested in him and Cody. Still, he couldn't shake the unease prickling his skin.

Movement across the street caught his attention. A guy in a hoodie emerged from between two buildings. He was of medium height and wore dark sunglasses and jeans. The stranger paused and glanced Henry's way before sauntering in the opposite direction.

Rubbing the back of his neck to dispel the unnerving sensation, he headed inside the building with Cody at his heels and went straight to tech guru Eden Chang's desk.

She blinked up at him. "Henry, what is this I hear about a text and a bomber?"

He handed over his phone and explained the situation.

Eden scratched Cody behind the ears. "You're a hero, boy." She took the device from Henry and plugged it into her computer console. "I'll do what I can. If the bomber used a burner phone to text you, then we won't get too much information. Unless it's still on, then I can ping it for a location. And I can definitely check the unique identifier number to learn where it was bought. And from there determine if we can find the person who made the purchase. But let's hope it's somebody's personal phone and they're too dumb to realize that the police can trace it."

Henry chuckled. "I couldn't be that fortunate."

She grinned at him. "Well, it's worth praying about."

"This is true." And he would be praying mightily. "Any breakthroughs on recovering anything off my body camera from the incident in Owl's Head Park?" He appreciated all the extra time Eden had put in on that.

She frowned. "No. Nothing more than what I had before. There's clear video of you walking into the park and clear video of you leaving the park. But the in-between is fuzzy."

"That is interesting and disturbing." The

one piece of evidence that would clear him of the excessive abuse charge.

"Exactly my thought. I still maintain that if a strong enough electromagnet got close enough to your body cam, it could cause this issue." Eden's intense gaze met his. "I believe you're being set up."

His stomach clenched at the disturbing idea that someone had gone to a lot of trouble to orchestrate a setup like this. If only he could talk to Davey Carrell himself and coax the guy into being honest about what happened. But Henry was going to have to rely on Olivia to ferret out the truth. "I wish you would tell Lieutenant Vance that."

Eden nodded once again, reaching to scratch Cody in his sweet spot. The dog leaned into her. "I told Lieutenant Jabboski and I will tell Lieutenant Vance when I talk with her. She left a message earlier today asking if we could meet."

"Thank you." It was good to have someone else on his side. "Hey, so about that bombing this afternoon… Can you pull up any video footage from around the entrance to

Coney Island, Luna Park, along the board-walk and the Joey Yums restaurant? At least two hours before the bomb detonated and maybe another two hours after. You know bombers, they tend to hang around to view their handiwork and the damage they've done."

"I'll work on it over the weekend," she promised.

He hated that she was going to give up her personal time for this, but it was a priority. "I really appreciate that."

"No sweat."

"Thanks." He gave her a salute. "I look forward to learning what you find out for me on Monday."

"Have a good weekend, you two," Eden said as she turned her attention to his phone.

Henry and Cody walked out of the tech room and into the station office. The place was pretty empty. There was a light on in Bradley McGregor's cube. Henry made Cody stay on the dog bed at his cubicle before heading to see his friend. Bradley's dog, King, a large Belgian Malinois, laid curled on a round bed. King lifted his head to watch as Henry stepped in to the cubicle. The tall, muscular detective swung around and smiled. "Heard you had an eventful day."

"You could say that."

"At least you, Riley and… Lieutenant Vance, are safe."

Ignoring the subtle ribbing in Bradley's tone, Henry said. "That's true." He'd never forget the relief that had flooded him when he'd realized Olivia was unharmed after the explosion. "What about you and Penny? How are you two holding up?"

The siblings had had a tragic childhood and there had been a recent double homicide that matched the modus operandi as the murders of their parents twenty years to the day. The brother and sister were understandably rattled.

Bradley took a breath. "Some days are better than others. I'm worried about Penny, though. She's taking it hard. Especially with another little girl being left alive at the scene."

Just as Penny had been left alive as a

young child when her parents had been brutally murdered. The killer had dressed as a blue-haired clown and given each little girl a stuffed monkey in a plastic bag.

Bradley had been at a sleepover with friends at the time of his parents' deaths. Back in the day, the police had considered Bradley a suspect and that he'd snuck home and killed his mother and father because the then fourteen-year-old had been outspoken about how negligent they'd been toward four-year-old Penny. That was never proven. Because it couldn't be true. To Henry, Bradley was as solid as they came. The unit was investigating both murders now.

"How's it going with the IA investigation?"

Henry blew out a compressed breath that left him a bit disoriented. "Honestly, I can't tell. When Lieutenant Vance first showed up this morning, she was ready to rumble. She believes that I'm capable of hurting someone without justification."

Bradley shook his head. "Man, I'd give

anything if we could go back and I could've just witnessed the altercation."

"You and me both, brother." Henry rubbed his chin as he debated his next words. "And I know this is going to sound totally bizarre and like I'm losing it, but I believe somebody's been following me."

Bradley stood, radiating tension. "Listen to your gut. It will never steer you wrong. Sometimes God talks to us in a small voice and sometimes in the loud clanging of a bell. You've got to honor it."

"I hear you, man." Henry had often listened to what he believed in his heart to be God directing him. Was that the case here?

Bradley clapped Henry on the back. "Anything I can do to help?"

Appreciating his friend's offer, Henry said, "I'll let you know."

"I'm here for you." Bradley leashed King and they left for the night.

Henry made quick work of writing up his report about the exploding garbage can while Cody ate his kibble. After a quick stroll on the grassy area between the unit headquarters and the training center next door, Henry kenneled Cody in the training center and then headed to Sal's.

From the doorway, he saw his sister and Olivia seated in the back corner. Their heads were bent close as they talked. He took a moment to study this woman who'd inserted herself into his life. What was her story?

He'd heard her sister Ally ask about "the baby" at Coney Island. He'd wanted to ask Olivia about her pregnancy, but then decided not to delve into her life. Better to not become emotionally embroiled with the IA investigator, no matter how attractive he found her. Because whether he liked it or not, she literally held the fate of his career in her hands. And any sort of personal relationship between them was strictly forbidden. Not that he was looking for a relationship. Especially not with a superior officer. They'd probably be hauled over the coals as it was for this innocent jaunt to the pizzeria. It bothered him that he had to second guess his every move.

"Hey, Roarke, what's IA doing with your sister?"

The question stopped Henry midstride as he made his way through the Friday night crowd at Sal's. His neck muscles braced as if taking a blow. He noted his sister pick up a carrot and dip it in dressing before taking a bite. Hmm. She wasn't one to normally eat veggies. Had that been Olivia's doing? He'd have to thank her.

With effort, he turned his attention to the man who'd asked the question. Henry tipped his chin to his colleague, Emergency Services officer Jackson Davison. "Jackson."

The imposing man sat at the counter. His green eyes were narrowed on Olivia. For some reason, irritation swept through Henry. He didn't understand his reaction to Jackson's query but wasn't about to analyze the emotion. "Looks like Lieutenant Vance is eating."

Jackson's gaze shot to Henry. "Obviously. But why? I thought she was investigating you."

Acid churned in Henry's stomach. "She is." The admission rankled. He couldn't wait for this debacle to be over. He'd always worked hard to be one of the good guys. His reputation was important to him and now it had been sullied.

"You better be careful," Jackson warned. "Riley might say something that the Lieutenant could use against you."

Drawing back, Henry stared at his fellow K-9 handler. "Like what?"

Jackson's eyebrows rose. "Like you have a temper."

Flexing his fingers, Henry made a face. "Ha. Just because I called foul on your play at the last basketball pickup game doesn't mean I have a temper."

Jackson grinned. "Dude, you threw a basketball through a window."

Grimacing, Henry said, "Purely accidental."

It was true he'd had a bad day on the court and had let a spike of anger get the better of him. In his defense, he'd just been put on modified duty and his sense of justice was riled up. It wasn't fair that Davey Carrell's unsubstantiated claim could cost Henry his job.

Shrugging, Jackson turned back to his

slice of pizza. "I'm just saying. If it were me under IA's microscope, I wouldn't be fraternizing with the enemy or let her anywhere near my family."

He clapped Jackson on the back. "Yeah, thanks."

As Henry moved through the restaurant, he noticed more people giving Olivia the eye. He wanted to tell everyone to mind their own business. She had just as much right to be in Sal's as anyone else. She'd paid her dues on the force before moving to Internal Affairs. Though he understood the need for oversight, most officers operated under the assumption that Internal Affairs rejoiced in taking down other officers. Unfortunately, there was no way he could dismiss decades of distrust between officers and IA. The fact that he wanted to defend Olivia didn't sit well. Her goal was to prove his guilt. Why did he care if she was treated with wariness and resentment?

Because she'd been nice to his sister. And had understood how important it had been for him to find Riley at Coney Island today.

Olivia had shown compassion and concern. She was human, after all, not just a robot out to find fault.

Shaking off his disturbing thoughts, he slid onto a stool beside his sister and took a carrot stick. "Ladies."

"Our pizzas should be ready any moment," Olivia said.

"Pizzas as in two?" He assessed the two women. Both were healthy and vibrant, but he doubted they'd eat that much. "Hungry, are we?"

Riley pointed the end of her carrot at Olivia. "Her idea."

Olivia shrugged. "Leftovers for tomorrow."

"Ah." Henry smiled. "That's reasonable."

"I can be reasonable," Olivia stated, her gaze direct.

"Glad to hear it," he countered, holding her gaze and pondering the defensive tone in her voice. He could only imagine the kind of flak she received doing her job. And the fortitude it took to accept that hostility.

"Vance, your pies are ready," a deep voice called out.

"I'll get them," Riley offered, sliding off her stool and hurrying to the counter.

Henry waved his hand at the salad and stack of carrot sticks sitting on the table. "Thanks for this, Olivia."

She slid the large salad bowl toward him and handed him a plate and fork. "Help yourself."

"Thank you for getting Riley to eat carrots."

"I know a thing or two about coaxing kids to eat their veggies. Smother them in dressing."

A small smile played at the corners of her lush mouth, drawing his attention. It hit him like a subway car that she was not just a lieutenant in Internal Affairs who could end his career, but a tempting, beautiful woman. The last thing he needed in his life right now. Not to mention becoming entangled with Olivia would put them both at risk of losing their jobs and being publicly repri-manded.

Forcing his gaze to the task of putting salad on his plate, he said, "You're one of six kids, right?"

"I am."

Sensing her gaze, he said, "I have just the one."

"One what?" Riley asked as she set the two pizzas on the table.

"We're talking about siblings," Olivia said. "I have two older brothers and three younger sisters."

"Wow." Riley grabbed a slice of Canadian bacon and pineapple and plopped it on her plate. "That's a lot. I couldn't handle more than Henry."

Henry shot his sister a mock glare. "Excuse me? Who has to handle who?"

Olivia's soft chuckle settled in his chest. He liked the sound of her laugh. As the evening progressed, Henry settled back, enjoying the way Riley and Olivia were hitting it off. Riley needed a female influence in her life. Raising a teenage girl alone had been difficult and if not for the advice of his female coworkers, he didn't know how he and Riley would have survived.

After eating their fill of pizza and chatting about the latest superhero movies, Henry had the remaining slices boxed up. One box for Olivia and one for him and Riley.

Outside of Sal's, Henry turned to Olivia. "Are you parked close?"

"I didn't drive," she said. "I'll call a car service."

His sense of honor and duty wouldn't allow him to accept that. Leaving her waiting on the street corner was unacceptable. "Can we give you a ride home?"

She hesitated a moment. "Actually, that would be great. I live in Carroll Gardens."

"Let me collect Cody and we'll be set to go." He led the way as Jackson's warning about trusting Olivia rang inside his brain. Was he making a mistake that could cost him his job?

THREE

With her hunger satisfied, Olivia marveled at the turn of events. When she'd arrived at the Brooklyn K-9 Unit earlier today, she'd expected to question Henry and then move on to meet with the unit's technology specialist, Eden Chang, to find out if there was video footage near Owl's Head Park that could help her track down as many of the young people who'd been at the skate park the evening of the incident involving Henry and Davey Carrell. Lieutenant Jabboski hadn't believed tracking down anyone from that night in the park was worth his time.

She still needed to meet with Miss Chang, but that would have to wait until next week. After surviving an exploding garbage can, conducting her interview near the roller coaster on Coney Island and eating nearly a whole pizza, Olivia only wanted to get home to change out of her clothes and put her feet up. Though having dinner with Henry and Riley certainly beat eating leftover pot roast alone.

After swiping his keycard on the security pad, Henry held the door of the training center open for Olivia and Riley to enter. Olivia had never set foot in the building before and was surprised by the cleanliness of the facility. She followed Henry and his sister into a large room that housed multiple hard-sided kennels. A few were occupied but the majority of the thirteen crates were empty.

A woman with shoulder-length auburn hair and brown eyes behind silver-framed glasses greeted them with a smile. "Cody's been sleeping, but I'm sure he's ready to go outside."

She opened the kennel door and the beagle shot out and raced to Riley. She knelt down and accepted slobbery kisses with a laugh.

Olivia watched the exchange with a pang of tenderness. Clearly, the dog and young woman were bonded, though in a different way then Henry and Cody. Watching the two in action today had been impressive.

"Gina, this is Lieutenant Olivia Vance," Henry said. "Dr. Gina Mazelli is our vet in residence."

Olivia shook the other woman's hand. "It's nice to meet you. Do you always work this late?"

"Likewise. I'm living in the building temporarily. We had a stray German shepherd give birth to five puppies in April. I'm fostering them and figured it would be best to keep them here. The mama, Brooke, is going to be trained for service. We'll see about the pups."

"I admire your dedication," Olivia said.

Gina shrugged. "I love animals."

"It shows." Olivia respected the other woman's devotion.

"Could we show Olivia the puppies?" Riley's hopeful expression was contagious. "They are so cute."

Excitement danced in Olivia's chest. "Would that be allowed?"

With an easy smile, the redheaded veterinarian nodded. "Of course it's allowed. The puppies need to be socialized."

Gina led the way to a small room where an extra-large dog exercise pen had been set up and cushioned with colorful blankets. The mama German shepherd reclined in the middle of the five little fur balls.

A couple of the puppies slept, while the other three roamed around the space. Olivia's heart swelled with tenderness.

Soon she'd have her own little one to cuddle. Her arms ached to hold her infant. There was so much she was looking forward to about being a mother. Reading to her child and teaching her little one to sing, to read and to dance with joy.

The future stretched before her and yet she had no idea how she was going to manage once she gave birth. Her parents had offered to help. But Olivia wanted to be there for every moment of her baby's life, from crawling to walking across the stage at her or his high school graduation.

She wasn't going to miss any firsts or special moments. She just hadn't figured out how to make it all work yet. She would, though. That was a promise she made to her baby the day she learned she was pregnant.

Riley went down on her hands and knees and crawled toward the pen, drawing Olivia's focus.

"Hello, you little cuties," Riley cooed.

Gina opened the wire gate so Riley could enter the pen. "Brooke, let's get you some food."

Brooke rose and gingerly stepped over the puppies, pausing to lick Riley's face before following Gina out of the room.

The runt of the litter stumbled on wobbly legs toward Riley. She scooped the pup into her arms and nuzzled him. "Hi, Maverick. It's good to see you again. You're going do great things. I just know it."

Olivia noted the sad wince pulling at Henry's expression. "What's wrong?"

"Maverick's life has been touch and go.

Still is, truth be told," he said in a low voice. "The little pup is frail and has health issues. But he's getting the best care possible. He has a fighting spirit."

"Come on, Olivia, hold a puppy," Riley called.

"Go on. They won't bite." He wagged his eyebrows. "Much."

She wrinkled her nose at him and then moved closer, sitting on the floor. Riley handed her Maverick. The tiny body quivered in her hands. She lifted him to look into his dark eyes. "It's okay. I've got you." She pulled him to her chest. Another puppy, twice the size of Maverick, crawled up her leg. She laughed, reaching out to stroke the soft fur.

Cody nuzzled his way into the pen to sniff the puppies, who pawed playfully at him.

Henry folded his frame to take a seat next to Olivia. He scooped up a puppy trying to escape. "Oh no, you don't."

"What will happen to them?" Olivia asked.

"Each will be tested soon to see if they'd be good working dogs or therapy dogs."

"And if they aren't?" She stroked her hand over Maverick. The pup had settled against her and seemed to be content in her arms. Would this be what it felt like to hold her child? Tenderness swelled in her chest and an ache of longing to protect this puppy, and the child growing inside of her, burned the back of her eyes.

"I'm sure Gina will find them homes."

The urge to take Maverick home with her pulsed in her veins. She wasn't set up to care for a puppy, or a baby, yet. But soon. She needed to put together the crib she'd ordered online, as well as the changing table and wash all the little clothes her family had been buying in neutral colors. She wasn't sure if she hoped for a girl or boy. Honestly, she didn't have a preference.

With Maverick's warm body snuggled against her chest, Olivia relaxed and a yawn escaped. Cody came over and nuzzled the puppy before giving Olivia a quick swipe of his tongue as if in approval. She couldn't help the laugh that escaped her.

"Ready to leave, Lieutenant?" Henry

asked, his gaze bouncing between his partner and her as if he were surprised by the dog's behavior.

Though Olivia didn't want to admit it, fatigue was setting in. The stress of the day had taken a toll. Her emotions were rubbed raw. She'd let down her guard and become comfortable with him. "Yes. Thank you, Henry."

They put the puppies back in the pen, latching the gate so they wouldn't escape. They said goodbye to Gina on the way out.

When they left the center, Cody was put in his compartment and Riley climbed in back of the SUV while Henry opened the side passenger door for Olivia. She smiled her gratitude and slid on to the seat, putting the pizza box on the floor at her feet. She appreciated he'd offered to drive her home. She doubted many officers who were being investigated would be so solicitous. It spoke volumes about his character.

When Henry settled in the driver's seat, he handed her his phone, open to the maps app. "Punch in your address, please, Olivia."

Too tired to argue and say she could just as easily tell him how to get there, she put her address into the device and handed it back. He pressed Start and a British female voice emanated from the phone, giving him directions. Thirty minutes later, he pulled up in front of her building, a four-story brick structure built in the 1920s.

When he moved to get out, she put her hand on his forearm. Warmth radiated up her arm and wrapped around her. She quickly drew her hand back. "You don't need to walk me in."

This wasn't a date, though she suspected his gesture stemmed from the overprotectiveness she'd seen glimpses of rather than some gallant offer of chivalry. Besides, she could take care of herself and her unborn child. She didn't need his or anyone else's protection.

Well, except her family...but that was different. Family helped each other out. Stuck together. She wished someone had told Roger that before he betrayed their marriage vows.

A frown showed Henry's concern and warmed her from the inside out. She had to admit he made her feel cared for, even though both were aware how dangerous forming any emotions for each other could be for their careers.

"We'll wait for you to enter the building," he said. "Which apartment is yours?"

She pressed her lips together to suppress the amusement of being proven right. He had a wide streak of chivalry. Even for someone he undoubtedly considered the enemy. Deciding to go with it and appreciate his thoughtfulness rather than cling to her independence, she said, "Bottom right. I'll wave from the window."

He gave a satisfied nod. "Okay. Good night, Olivia."

"Good night, Henry." She popped open the door and found Riley waiting to take her place in the front seat. "It was really nice to meet you, Riley."

"You, too," the younger woman said. "I hope I see you again."

Taking one of her business cards from her

suit jacket pocket, Olivia held it out. "My cell phone is on this. You call me if you ever need anything. Even if it's just to chat."

Riley palmed the card. "Thank you."

As Olivia withdrew her hand, Cody let out a soft bark.

Riley laughed. "He says good-night, too."

Smiling, Olivia hurried to unlock the building's front entrance, then went to her apartment door and unlocked the double bolt that her father had installed when she'd moved in right after Roger's death. She hadn't wanted to stay in the ultra-modern condo they had shared. Too many memories, most of which she didn't want to keep.

Once inside her small one-bedroom unit, she secured the door, flipped on the lights and went to the window. Drawing back the curtain, she waved at the vehicle idling at the curb. Henry waved back before driving the SUV away.

A stark and cold sense of isolation invaded her, making her insides quiver. Not since the night her late husband had stormed out of her life had she felt so alone.

But soon there would be a little bundle of joy for her to love. Until then, she had to deal with the loneliness disturbing her sense of peace.

With a sigh, she dropped the curtain and faced her apartment. The quiet surrounded her, unnerving in its completeness.

"Kitty?"

A soft meow came from the bedroom. Her faithful companion couldn't be bothered to come greet her. Maybe she *should* get a dog.

Henry pulled away from the Carroll Gardens apartment building. He kept an eye on the curtain of Olivia's window as it fluttered closed. She had moved away from view. He didn't like leaving her knowing she was alone. He'd heard about the death of her husband, but it hadn't seemed quite the appropriate topic to discuss. Not that he wanted to discuss it. He didn't want to get involved with this woman. She was an irritation. A burr under his flak vest. Even if he did feel sympathy for her loss and had, surprisingly, enjoyed her company tonight.

Watching her with Riley and having Cody give her his stamp of approval with the lick at the training center created conflicting emotions within him. There was something so very vulnerable about Olivia. Yet formidable, too.

Maybe it was the fact that he suspected she was pregnant, if what her sister had said was true. Or that Olivia was a widow, still grieving her late husband. Or maybe it was the stress of the day getting to him, stirring up uncomfortable feelings he had no business entertaining. She was a superior officer and investigating him. How much more taboo could any feelings for Olivia be?

Yes, it had to be the stress of the day or the blow to his head.

Well, more like the stress of the past three, almost four months, to be exact. Ever since the night Davey Carrell tried to grab Henry's sidearm. The ever-present frustration reared as Henry merged into traffic, heading toward their Cobble Hill neighborhood. Bright headlights moved in behind the SUV, causing apprehension to slither over his flesh.

His paranoia was getting the better of him. On the way to Olivia's apartment there had been a moment when he'd suspected they were being followed. But the silver sedan had veered away and turned down a side street. Then the car reappeared at the next block, turning into the driveway of a parking garage a half block past Olivia's apartment. Clearly, he was losing it.

But as he drove into his neighborhood, he was sure the car behind him was the same silver sedan that had been tailing him since he left Olivia's apartment. Just to make sure, he went right at the stoplight and headed away from the street where his two-story condo was located.

"Where are we going?" Riley asked.

Watching the rearview mirror, Henry replied, "Just circling the block."

He was halfway down the block when the silver sedan made the turn.

Heart rate doubling, Henry turned down another block. Sure enough, the car followed. As they passed beneath the illuminating glow of a streetlamp, he caught a better glimpse of the silver sedan and the empty space where the front license plate should have been. Tensing, he made another quick turn.

"Henry?"

Not wanting to scare his sister, he said, "Being cautious."

Who was driving the sedan? Why was he, or Riley, being targeted? Did this have something to do with Davey Carrell? He tightened his grip until his knuckles hurt. Rounding the block, he kept a vigilant eye on the rearview mirror. The sedan didn't follow.

Shaking his head, he sped home and parked in his designated spot. He climbed out, retrieved Cody from his compartment and ushered Riley, along with the pizza box, up the steps to their condo. He made her wait at the front door while he and Cody cleared the place. Once he was satisfied there were no dangerous surprises waiting for them, he said, "We're good."

Silently handing him the pizza box, she headed to her room, but he'd glimpsed the anxiety in her dark eyes as she passed him.

His chest tightened. He'd do everything in his power to keep her safe. After letting Cody out in the small fenced-in side yard of the condo, Henry secured the premises for the night.

Too wired to sleep, he kept the lights off as he stood guard, pacing between the windows at the front of the condo and the ones lining the balcony. Cody whined, wanting Henry to go to bed. But he couldn't. He was going to listen to his gut. If it was God talking to him, he had every intention of paying attention.

In the wee hours of the morning, a low growl emanated from Cody, raising the fine hairs at the back of Henry's neck. He bolted upright from the living room recliner. When he reached the kitchen, he found Cody standing at attention in the moonlight streaming through the glass insert of the balcony door. His tail raised high, his ears back.

A shadow passed by the door, momentarily obscuring the ambient light.

Henry's heart jackknifed with adrenaline.

Someone was on the balcony.

FOUR

Heart hammering in his chest, Henry didn't want to alert the intruder as he spoke softly to Cody, "Good boy. No bark."

For a second, Henry debated retrieving his weapon from the gun safe in his bedroom. But it would take precious time and he wanted to act now. Hurrying to the hall closet, he grabbed his dad's Louisville Slugger. Hefting the bat in his hands and staying in the shadows, he returned to the kitchen. With Cody at his side, he approached the door leading to the balcony and quietly unlocked the door, then wrapped his hand around the knob.

On a deep breath, he yanked open the door and hit the light switch, throwing the five-foot-wide balcony into sharp relief. The platform, guarded by a wrought iron railing, ran the length of the condo's second floor. A medium-height, slender man wearing dark jeans, gloves and a black hoodie that cast his face in shadow stood outside the window to the room Henry used as an office.

"Halt, police!" Henry yelled and rushed toward the prowler. Cody scrambled past Henry, his teeth bared as he growled menacingly.

The hooded man dropped to a crouch for a split second as if he could hide before jumping to his feet. Cody latched on to his pant leg. With a vicious kick, the intruder dislodged Cody. The sound of fabric ripping filled the air as Cody tore away a chunk of the pants. Once free of Cody, the man grasped the railing with his gloved hands and swung over the side, dangling there for an instant before dropping away.

"No!" Henry reached the spot where the prowler had just been. Bracing himself, because he was positive the guy would have broken a leg or something from the fall, he leaned over the railing just in time to see the would-be burglar shimmying down the drainpipe to the ground below. "Hey!"

Without looking up, the man scaled the side yard fence and disappeared out of sight. Then his pounding footfalls echoed through the still night as he ran away. There was no way Henry would catch him. Frustration beat a steady rhythm at his temples. After checking that Cody hadn't sustained an injury from the kick, Henry darted back inside and called the precinct. He explained the situation to the night dispatcher.

"I'll alert patrol to be on the lookout for anyone matching that description," the dispatcher promised.

Doubting they'd catch the guy, Henry said, "Can you send a CSI team to my residence? Specifically Darcy Fields." She worked often with the K-9 team and was an ace forensic specialist. If there was any evidence that could lead to the intruder's identity she'd find it.

"Will do, Detective Roarke."

After hanging up, Henry went to wake Riley with Cody at his heels. He cracked opened her bedroom door, allowing the hall light to spill into the room and flinched at the mess. Clothes hung half out of her dresser drawers and shoes lay haphazardly on the floor like little traps for him to trip over. Stacks of books, six to ten high, appeared ready to topple if he so much as breathed on them. Her messiness was another source of contention between them. He didn't understand how Riley could operate in such chaos.

Carefully, he and Cody picked their way across the room to her full-size bed. She lay twisted in her covers, her sweet face relaxed and her arms wrapped around a large stuffed animal that Henry had won for her at Coney Island several years earlier.

Tenderness filled his chest as he sank onto the bed. Cody sat at his feet. "Hey, munchkin," he said, using the childhood nickname their father had coined when she was an infant.

She stirred, rolling to her side away from him. He gently nudged her.

"What?" she asked, though her eyes remained closed. "I'm sleeping."

"We have a situation," he said. "Someone tried to break in."

That grabbed her attention. She twisted to face him. Her dark eyes went wide as she blinked away sleep. "Break in?"

"A crime scene unit will be here soon," he told her. "You don't have to get up. I just didn't want you to be frightened if you woke up and heard noises."

"Are we safe?"

He smoothed back her hair. She looked so much like her mother, Susan. Henry had always liked his stepmom. She'd tried hard to forge a relationship with him, even though he'd been less than receptive until he'd become a young adult. "Yes. We're safe. But if you'd feel better I can leave Cody here with you."

"Don't you need him?"

"I'll be fine," he assured her. "He's already done his job tonight." For which Henry was grateful. Cody was better than an alarm system…but he might have one installed anyway.

Riley scooted over to make room for the dog. "Okay."

Henry patted the bed. Cody jumped up, sniffed at Riley and licked her face before turning in a circle and settling down beside her. Riley slipped her arms around Cody much the way she had been hugging the stuffed toy.

A sharp knock at the front door had Henry rising to his feet. "I'll let you know when they've gone." He reversed his trek through the minefield of her room, leaving Cody curled by her side.

At the front door, he greeted Darcy Fields, a petite blonde with pale brown eyes and dimples in her cheeks. She carried a case filled with her equipment and wore her uniform of khakis, dark blue polo shirt with the NYPD logo and dark shoes, now covered with paper booties. Her team of two male techs filled the space behind her.

"Hi, Darcy. You got here quick."

"We were just finishing up at a crime scene nearby when I received the call. Came straight here. Not much in the way of traffic at three o'clock in the morning." The forensic specialist led her team into the condo.

"I appreciate you coming," he said. "The prowler was on the balcony." He led the way through the condo. Stepping out to the terrace, he said, "He must have climbed up from below." He told her how the man had swung over the railing.

"Agile trespasser," she commented. "Was he wearing gloves?"

"Unfortunately, yes. But Cody snagged a piece of his pant leg." He pointed to the scrap of material on the ground where Cody had dropped it.

She quickly bagged the evidence, then turned to the two men with her. "Head to the ground level and see if you can find any footprints in the soft dirt of the flowerbed that we can use."

The two men nodded and retreated out the front door.

"I'll dust to see if there's any pattern in the grain of the gloves the suspect wore," Darcy said. "It may or may not be helpful. And I'll look for stray hairs or epithelia on the material. Let's pray we get a match in one of the many DNA databases."

"I should have tackled him," Henry muttered.

Darcy gave him a sharp glance. "Aren't you being investigated for excessive force?"

Henry flinched. "Yes." Though he didn't see what that had to do with this situation.

"Then it's probably better for you not to have any physical contact with a suspect," she said.

He grunted, not liking the accuracy of her statement. He had to trust that Darcy's crack skills would produce some evidence to lead to the intruder. But until the guy was caught and brought in, Henry would remain in the dark about why he had wanted into his house. What had he been planning to do?

Henry gazed out at the darkened street and vowed he'd do everything in his power to keep his sister safe.

The next morning, Henry awoke from of fitful rest. The only reason he'd been able to get any sleep was the assurance that two patrol officers were watching the condo building. After checking in with the officers and letting them know he was up and about and they could go have their day off, Henry made a strong pot of coffee. He didn't particularly like the stuff, but there were days when he needed it.

His head hurt where he'd sustained a gash from the flying debris after the garbage can explosion. He really needed to go see the doctor and have the bandage changed. But thankfully no blood had seeped through. That was a good sign.

He popped a couple of over-the-counter painkillers with some water as the coffee percolated. Just as he was pouring himself his first strong cup, he heard Riley's door open and the pad of Cody's feet coming down the hall. Leaving his coffee on the counter, he grabbed Cody's leash and collar from the basket near the front door.

"Here, boy." He opened the front door as Cody hurried up to his side and sat patiently waiting for him to put on his collar and lead. They went outside so Cody could have a few moments on the grass. The early morning air was just beginning to heat up with the promise of another hot July day. There were few people out and about. Saturdays were generally quiet. Still, Henry kept a vigilant eye out for any sign of the silver sedan or for strangers who didn't belong in the area.

When they returned to the apartment, Riley was dressed and making scrambled eggs. Henry unleashed Cody and made sure there was fresh water in the dog bowl. The dog sniffed at Riley's pink backpack sitting on the edge of the couch before jumping up on to the cushion and lying down. Henry wandered back to his cup of coffee, which had grown cold. He dumped it out and poured himself a fresh cup. He leaned back against the counter. "You're up early."

"Nicole called and woke me up," she replied with a quick glance. "We're making plans for the upcoming concert. We thought we'd get ready at Kelsey's place." Riley's expression turned hopeful. "You aren't really serious about going with us to and from the concert hall, are you?"

He rounded the corner of the counter and

sat back on his stool. "Dead serious. Especially now. With bomb threats and someone trying to break into our condo. We have to be vigilant and use caution."

Her shoulders slumped as she dished eggs onto plates. When she sat the plate in front of him, it bounced slightly with her agitation. "I'm eighteen. I don't need a babysitter. Nicole's nineteen and Kelsey's eighteen, like me. We're adults now. I don't need your permission. And I certainly don't need you as my shadow."

There was so much in her statement to unpack and pick apart, he couldn't decide where to start. "First off, you may be eighteen, but you live under my roof. When you move out and start adulting, I will have no say in your life. But until then, you have to abide by my rules."

She huffed and rolled her eyes. "That's so lame."

A flash of memory hit him along with a sense of déjà vu. Though he couldn't recount the exact words, he was certain he'd had a very similar conversation with their father when he was Riley's age. Arguing with her about this wouldn't be productive. So he chose to go with the more obvious issue. "We can't ignore the danger."

"What does that have to do with me? You're the cop, the one putting his life on the line. Not me. I'll be fine." She glared at him as she dredged up an old argument.

From the day she realized what his job entailed, Riley had resented his career. He understood from the grief counselor they'd both seen after the tragic death of their father and her mom that Riley's anger was a mask for the fear of losing him, too.

He rubbed a hand over his whiskered jaw. There was no delicate way to give her a reality check. "Did you forget what happened yesterday? You were within striking distance of a bomb."

He recalled Olivia's comment that it had been an unlikely coincidence that Riley was at Coney Island the same time as the bomber was texting Henry. Had the bomber known his sister was there? Had she been targeted? Or was it a strange fluke that they intersected? He wished he had answers to the questions plaguing him.

"I barely heard the explosion," she shot back.

Frustration tightened the muscles of his shoulders. He steered the conversation back to the original topic. "If you want to go to the concert," he said slowly, "This is what we are doing."

"It's not fair." She stabbed her fork into the fluffy eggs on the plate in front of her.

"Life is not fair, Riley. God never promised it would be. The sooner you get that through your head and accept it, the better. Because expecting life to be even and square will only frustrate you."

She set down her fork and stared at him with tears clouding her dark eyes. "You sound so much like Dad."

His heart twisted in his chest. Riley's grief was always near the surface, especially when they were arguing. But this was the first time she'd compared Henry to their father. Her words were both a compliment that made him proud and a wound that sliced him to the quick.

Their father, James Roarke, had been a man of integrity who'd provided a good life for his children as an accountant. Henry's mother had abandoned Henry and James when Henry was six, disappearing and never contacting her son again. For many years, it had just been Henry and his dad until his dad had met Susan Cantor. They'd married and soon had Riley.

Even as an infant, the little girl had had their father wrapped around her pinky.

Taking a bracing sip of coffee, Henry stalled a beat as he wrangled his own grief. Swallowing, he said, "Riley, I love you. But you're not going to that concert without an escort both to and from."

She threw up her hands. "That's just mean."

Holding on to his patience by a thread, he said, "Riley, it's not mean. It's being protective."

"You're smothering me." She grabbed her plate and scraped the last of her eggs into the disposal before setting the plate in the dishwasher. She slammed the dishwasher door shut.

Cody let out a startled bark and jumped off the couch. He trotted over to investigate the commotion while Riley moved into the living room. Her phone chimed with an incoming text. She glanced at it and rolled her eyes. Snagging her backpack from the couch, she said, "I have an anthropology assignment that's due Monday. I'm going to the Museum of Natural History."

He slapped a hand to his forehead. "You're not going to the museum by yourself. You're going to have to wait for me and I will take you."

"I don't need you to come with me."

He stood up, marshaling his frustration and irritation, and stared her down. "Riley, someone tried to break in last night. You're not going to win here."

"You're impossible." She stormed down the hall, slamming her bedroom door shut.

Henry slumped back onto the counter stool. He understood her desire for more freedom. He was exactly the same age when he left home for college. But times were different. Their father hadn't been a cop. Riley didn't understand that he couldn't risk her safety. He'd seen the worst of humanity. How did he make her understand that it wasn't her he didn't trust? It was everyone else.

He cradled his head in his hands and lifted up a prayer asking God for guidance and wisdom because he didn't know how to navigate this young adult stage. In fact, he wasn't sure he'd ever know how to do the parent thing. And had no plans to again. Raising Riley was enough for one lifetime.

Putting on her sunglasses, Olivia stepped out of her Saturday morning exercise class when her cell phone rang. She paused on the sidewalk to dig the device out of her bag. She glanced at the caller ID and didn't recognize the number. Hefting her rolled exercise mat beneath one arm and her gym bag over her shoulder, she stepped out of the flow of traffic into the alcove of a restaurant that wasn't open yet.

"Hello?"

She heard a sobbing hiccup and then a weepy female voice, "Olivia? I mean, Lieutenant Vance?"

The voice struck a familiar chord, but Olivia couldn't place it. "Yes, this is Lieutenant Olivia Vance."

"This is Riley, Riley Roarke."

Olivia's stomach clenched. "Is everything okay, Riley?"

"No, it's not. Henry's a tyrant. I just can't live like this anymore. Can you help me?"

The dire note in Riley's tone slid along Olivia's limbs. Henry wouldn't hurt Riley, would he? He seemed to dote on her. "Are you safe?"

"Yes. Will you come?"

What was going on? Had Henry lost his temper with his sister? Did Henry really have an anger issue? After yesterday, she'd started to think not. But now Olivia was doubting herself. She needed to make sure there was no credence to the excessive force allegations by seeing what Henry was like with his family at home, she decided. She took off at a fast clip toward her apartment. "Can you text me your address? I'll be right there."

"Okay, please hurry."

When the text came in from Riley, Olivia's eyebrows shot up when she saw the Cobble Hill address. Pretty swanky on a police officer's salary. How could Henry afford such a nice condo?

At home, she quickly freshened up and changed into work clothes. She exchanged her workout equipment for her purse and made sure Kitty had water, then hustled back out the door. Squaring her shoulders with determination to get to the bottom of what was going on, she called a car service. She lifted up a prayer that she would be able to diffuse whatever was going on.

FIVE

Henry returned from the doctor's office with a new bandage on his head and a prescription for pain pills that he wouldn't be taking. Over-the-counter pain medication would do just fine. He wasn't about to take something stronger that would impair his judgment. Not when there was so much at stake. His sister's life, his life and the safety of the neighborhood. The safety of Brooklyn.

Riley was still in her room, no doubt pouting, so he took Cody outside again. The late-morning July sun beat down on his head. Staying inside would be a good idea today. A perfect time to go with Riley to the museum.

Back inside the condo, Henry knocked on

Riley's door. "Hey, sis? I'm ready to go to the Museum of Natural History whenever you are."

"Whatever," came her muffled reply through the door.

Blowing out a frustrated breath, he shook his head. Was she really going to do this? She wanted to be treated like an adult, yet when she didn't get her way, she acted like she had at thirteen. Experience told him he had to wait her out. He headed back to the kitchen and finished loading the dishwasher, setting it to run. To keep himself busy, he wiped down the counters and cleaned out the fridge.

A knock at the front door set Cody scrambling from his bed. Tension constricted the muscles in Henry's neck as he hung back a second to watch his partner. Cody would give a passive alert indicating if a bomb waited on the other side of the door. The dog sniffed, then scratched at the door, apparently not detecting a dangerous scent.

Still, Henry used caution and pressed his eye to the peephole. Lieutenant Olivia

Vance stood on the other side, looking very professional in a black pantsuit and crisp white shirt.

He drew back in surprise and rubbed a hand over his stubbled jaw. He usually didn't shave on the weekends. Then he shrugged. She was at his house on a Saturday. She could hardly expect him to be uniform-ready. He opened the door and braced himself. "Olivia. What brings you to my house on a Saturday?"

Adjusting the strap of her purse on her shoulder, she took a moment to respond, as if collecting her thoughts. "I need to speak with Riley."

His gut knotted. "Why?"

Her gaze hardened. "Riley called me. I want to talk to her and make sure she's okay."

Henry groaned. "Seriously? She called you? I'm sorry she bothered you. We had an argument but after the attempted break-in last night—"

"Wait," Olivia held up a hand. "Someone tried to break in here?"

"Yes. But Cody alerted and the perpetrator ran away. And now Riley's upset at the restrictions I've set and she's being overly dramatic. It's what she does."

Olivia's face softened just a tad. "I'm glad to hear none of you were hurt. I'd like to see her, please."

With a sigh of aggravation, he stepped aside so the Internal Affairs lieutenant could enter his condo. "By all means. Come in."

She glanced around his space. Suddenly, uncharacteristic insecurities assailed him. Did she notice the stain on the carpet? The dust on the picture frames? The secondhand furniture he'd picked up at a yard sale? He was glad he'd at least cleaned up the kitchen area.

"Nice place." Her gaze landed on him. "How do you afford this on your salary?"

Taken aback by her direct question, he lifted an eyebrow. Apparently nothing was out of bounds for her. "It *is* nice. And it was paid for with the life insurance money from my father's estate."

Tenderness filled her eyes, making his heart skip a beat.

"It must have been very difficult for you and Riley."

"Yes. The pain is always just underneath the surface," he admitted, though why he'd tell her anything personal was beyond him. Maybe because he sensed she understood grief. "I was sorry to hear about the loss of your husband."

Sadness and another emotion he couldn't identify crossed her face. "Thank you."

Confused by the stiffness of her tone, he asked, "A small plane crash, correct?"

Her gaze shuttered. "Yes."

Did she feel guilty that she hadn't been with him at the time of his death? It wasn't unusual for those left behind to have survivor's guilt. "You must miss him."

For a moment, she was quiet, as if debating how to answer. "At times. We were married for only two years. Our careers didn't lend themselves to married life."

His eyebrows rose as he digested her statement. "What was his profession?"

"A dentist," she said. "He had a thriving practice."

There was just a hint of bitterness in her tone that raised his curiosity. Though he really shouldn't pry, he asked, "Where was he headed when he crashed?"

For a moment she didn't speak and he cringed. He had overstepped. "I'm sorry, Olivia. It's none of my business."

"It's not a secret. From what I was told, the Caribbean," she replied. "We weren't on speaking terms at the time." She clamped her lips together as if she hadn't meant to let the admission slip.

Stunned by that revelation, Henry wasn't sure how to respond. Empathy flooded him. He fought the need to soothe away the hurt lurking in her eyes. Doing so would definitely be out of bounds.

Riley opened her bedroom door and ran straight at Olivia, throwing her arms around the woman. "You came!"

Olivia's eyes went wide and her mouth opened in obvious surprise. She braced her feet apart to balance herself against the onslaught of the gangly teenager. Henry winced. His little sister was putting on quite a show.

Olivia pulled back to look into Riley's face. "What's going on?"

Riley hitched a thumb over her shoulder. "Him. He's a brute."

Henry's mouth fell open. Didn't his little sister understand that saying things like that to the officer investigating him for excessive force would hurt his career? But then again, he figured hurting him was her intent. Riley wasn't getting her way and she was acting out. Not cool at all.

Letting out a half groan, half sigh, he shook his head and walked toward the balcony door. "I'll let you two talk."

Hopefully, Olivia was smart enough to realize what was going on and not hold Riley's antics against him.

Olivia saw the play of emotions march across Henry's face before he turned away. Obviously, his sister's words were upsetting to him. From the moment Olivia had stepped inside the condo, she'd had trouble keeping her focus on why she'd come over. Henry was breathtakingly handsome today.

She'd always thought him good-looking in uniform. But dressed in khaki shorts and a short-sleeve, pale green button-down shirt, he appeared both casual and dressy at the same time. He had a crisp, white bandage on his head that was a stark reminder of the trauma they'd experienced together.

A bond that had led her to admit she and her late husband hadn't been on speaking terms. Why else would she reveal anything personal to an officer she was investigating? She pushed aside the persistent voice that whispered she liked this man.

Leaving the door open to the balcony, Henry settled onto a deck chair with his back to them. Cody lay down beside him. Henry dangled his hand over the armrest and stroked Cody as if needing comfort. Which Olivia figured he probably did, considering his sister's state of mind.

Turning her attention to Riley, Olivia met the younger woman's red-rimmed gaze. Remembering well the emotional roller coaster her two younger sisters had trapped the family on when they were young adults, Olivia decided to tread softly. Leading Riley to the leather couch, she said, "Tell me what's going on."

Riley plopped down on the middle cushion, tucking her feet beneath her and giving a very beleaguered sigh. "He's just so overprotective. He's a helicopter parent."

Olivia pressed her lips together to keep a smile at bay because showing any sort of amusement would only lead to more drama. At least, it always had with her siblings. "And what is he being an overprotective helicopter parent about?"

"The Colt Colton concert is coming up at the Barclays Center and he insists on escorting me and my friends."

Ah. So that was the crux of the issue. Taking Riley's hand in her own, Olivia gave her a gentle squeeze. "You do realize he's acting out of love? Especially after an intruder trying to break in."

For a moment, Riley's mouth firmed into

a stubborn line, then she seemed to deflate. "I know. I know he loves me. And last night was scary. But he won't even let me go to the Natural Museum of History today by myself. I'm eighteen, old enough to go into the city on my own. I have an anthropology project due on Monday and I'm supposed to go to the museum and pick a subject to write about. We can't do it online. The teacher said we actually have to go to the museum. I don't want Henry to go with me. My other classmates will be there. I'll die if I have to have my big brother tagging along."

Dizzy from the onslaught of words, Olivia held up a hand. "Again, you do realize he's trying to protect you because he loves you?"

Riley threw herself against the backrest of the couch, her gaze on the ceiling. "Yes."

At least the young woman was acknowledging the truth through her dramatics.

Suddenly, Riley sat straight up and stared at Olivia. "Will you come with us? If you're with him, then he won't be hovering over me. You two can go off and do your own thing." She flicked her fingers as if shooing away a fly. "But he can still be there in case I need him."

From the balcony, Henry called out, "I'm okay with that."

Astonished, Olivia stared at the back of Henry's head. Really? He was okay with her going to the museum with him and his sister? Hmm. No doubt he wanted a buffer between him and Riley, too.

Was she seriously contemplating letting herself be drawn into this family's drama?

Who was she kidding? The moment she'd agreed to come over, she'd stepped into the fray. And she could be of help here. She wanted to help the brother and sister figure out how to navigate this season they were in. After all, she did have the knowledge and training. Plus, seeing them interact more outside of the home would help her understand the dynamics between them. She smiled wryly. "I'm ready to go whenever you are."

Riley clapped her hands and jumped from the couch. "I'll grab my backpack."

Henry came back inside and stopped at

the foot of the couch. His gaze searched her face. "Are you sure about this?"

Misgivings filled Olivia, but she wasn't one to go back on her word. "Yes."

Henry leashed Cody and slipped a K-9 Unit vest over his small, round body.

"You're taking your partner?"

"It's a perfect opportunity to do some real world training. Besides, better to be prepared in case the texting bomber strikes again."

A shiver rippled over her flesh. She couldn't argue with that logic.

The trek into the city via the subway was uneventful. Riley buried her head in her phone, apparently texting with her classmates. Henry remained standing the whole ride, his gaze hard as he studied each passenger. Cody sniffed everyone he passed but showed no signs of alerting.

Seated next to Riley, Olivia fretted more with every mile that clicked beneath the rails. A bubbly sensation in her belly made her wonder if the baby sensed her anxiety. She breathed deep in an effort to calm herself and the baby. Yet her mind nagged at her—what if somebody from one of the precincts saw the four of them and realized they were on an outing together?

She could claim this was work-related, though would anyone believe her? She hated to acknowledge it, but she was jeopardizing her own career by fraternizing with the officer she was investigating.

However, it was her day off, even if she was treating it like work. A rebellious streak she rarely let loose clamored that today she was not an Internal Affairs investigator. Today, she was just a woman accompanying a teenager and her older brother and his dog to visit the museum. Nothing more. And if anybody actually bought that rationalization, she had a really nice piece of swampland in the middle of Manhattan to sell them.

With her stomach tied in knots, she followed Henry, Cody and Riley off the train and to the entrance of the American Museum of Natural History.

Bypassing the electronic ticket kiosks,

Henry stepped up to the ticket counter, showed his badge and explained that he and Cody would be doing some training.

The ticket agent shrugged.

"Two adult and one student," Henry said.

Oh no, he was not going to buy her ticket. That would definitely be crossing a line. Olivia put her hand on his arm. "I can pay my own way."

He frowned but nodded and turned back to the ticket agent. "One adult, one student, then."

The agent handed Henry his tickets and then stared expectantly at Olivia. She dug into her purse and produced the right amount of cash for her ticket.

"You really didn't have to buy your ticket," Henry said. "You're doing us a favor by being here."

Riley linked her arms through Olivia's and Henry's as they moved past the ticket counter. Wedged between them, her gaze bounced back and forth. "That's right, Olivia. You're doing Henry and me a great favor. When we get inside, you two take

Cody and just toddle off in the opposite direction of me, okay?"

Henry shook his head. "Uh, no."

Riley detached herself from them with a huff.

Olivia spoke up. "We will stay discreetly in the background. Won't we, Henry?"

"Yes, we will," he said. "We'll stay within striking distance."

Riley halted. "No, no, no. You have to stay at least thirty feet behind me."

Olivia laughed. "We can do that."

"Hey," Henry said. "I'm not sure about that."

Olivia's tucked her arm through Henry's. "Henry, we need to chat about a little thing called letting go."

Henry's heart hiccupped. *Okay, Lord, so this is your answer?* He eyed Olivia. For her to bring up the subject of letting go, after he'd prayed earlier that morning asking God for direction on how to let Riley grow up, had Henry's mind reeling. He tightened his hold on Cody's leash. The dog, attuned to

Henry, stared up at him as if questioning what had his handler upset.

Henry took a shuddering breath and tried to reduce the storm raging within him. Purposely, he relaxed his hold on the leash, giving Cody more slack.

Riley picked up speed, heading into the nearest exhibit. Henry guided Cody and Olivia in his sister's wake. So far Cody hadn't caught any scents that he associated with explosives.

Before they stepped into the exhibit room his sister had entered, Olivia put pressure on his arm, forcing him to stop. "You need to give her some space."

"Olivia, how exactly do I do that with some maniac out there who set off a bomb while she was in the vicinity and then someone tries to break in?" A chill of residual fear swept down his back. If something had happened to Riley, he didn't know if he could survive.

"We have to trust that God will keep her safe and give you the means to protect her."

He drew in a breath, glad to hear she

trusted God. In this moment it was easy to forget she was IA. He hadn't realized he needed a friend with whom he could discuss the situation. "You're right. But sometimes it's so hard to do."

"Agreed. Believe me, when you have an issue with control, faith can be a challenge."

"You, too?"

She gave him a sheepish smile. "Oh, yes. More than I care to admit. We'll walk in there in just a moment and we'll be able to keep an eye on her. Really, Henry, she *is* eighteen. You're treating her like she's six."

He ground his back teeth. "Now you're going to start in on me? I can't help it. There's no playbook for me to consult. I'm doing the best I can."

"And you're doing a great job. I know it's hard," she said. "Being stuck in the middle of my siblings with two very busy parents, I took care of my sisters and corralling my older brothers."

"Your brothers are both really good friends of mine. You did a good job with those two. I only know Ally on an acquaintance level. I haven't met your other two sisters. Though I've heard the one in the DA's office is—" He stopped, searching for a polite way convey what he'd been told.

Olivia laughed. "Maria is a shark. It's okay. I know. Even as a kid, she had a strong sense of justice and the determination to make the world a better place."

There was affection in her tone and he smiled. He liked this side of her. "I don't know if I could ever go through this again."

"You don't want children of your own one day?"

He shrugged. "I hate to say never but right now, no, I don't."

She looked away and appeared fascinated by the plaque on the wall. There was a tension in her shoulders that hadn't been there before.

Not sure what he'd said to upset her, he nudged her. "Okay, so what kind of wisdom do you want to impart to me?"

She started them walking in the direction that Riley had disappeared. Henry scanned the exhibit room and caught a glimpse of his sister as she read the plaque for a display.

Olivia stopped him so that they could pretend to view an exhibit on sea turtles. "Henry, here's the thing. There's a fine line between letting go and giving up. You don't want to give up. That's not okay. That's how many teens and young adults end up in trouble. But letting go means you stop treating her like a child."

He opened his mouth to protest, but Olivia held up a hand. "I don't mean that you shouldn't protect her from imminent and real danger. But you have to stop rescuing her. She's in college now. It's time for her to take responsibility."

"I get what you're saying but sometimes when I look at her, I still see that scared, traumatized twelve-year-old."

"Becoming the parent of a preteen overnight must have been very hard for you. Now, you have to transition to being a marvelous big brother who lets his little sister grow up and make mistakes."

He nodded as he digested her words.

Could he be a brother and not a parent? He had no idea how to go about making that sort of switch in his thinking now. Especially with the threat of a bomber targeting their little family unit.

Riley moved on to another exhibit. After a several moments, they entered into the large mammal section. Riley was about fifteen feet away, looking at the mummified remains of baby woolly mammoth. The two girls who'd been with her at Coney Island had joined her.

Stopping to look at the fossil display of a Lestodon, he said to Olivia, "You must've been a real blessing to your parents."

Her mouth quirked. "I hope so."

"You're good at this, you know."

She arched an eyebrow. "At what?"

"Giving out wise counsel. And the way you dealt with Riley... I was impressed. If you hadn't joined the force, you'd make a wonderful guidance counselor."

An expression mixed between pain and surprise crossed Olivia's face before her attention shifted away from him. Why did his praise upset her?

"Who's that talking to your sister?"

His gaze landed on a young man not much older than Riley. All of Henry's senses went on alert as he recognized the expression of panic on Riley's face.

In long strides, with Cody close at his heels, Henry reached Riley's side in time to hear her say, "I've already told you, I can't. Please, stop asking me."

"What's going on here?" Henry asked, planting his feet wide, his hands at his sides, ready to drop Cody's leash and scrabble with this kid if he didn't back down. Cody sniffed at the younger guy and lost interest.

The young man turned dark eyes on Henry. There was a flash of disdain in his gaze before he stepped back and held up his hands, palms out. "Hey, sorry. I go to school with Riley. No harm. I was just asking her some questions."

"What's your name?" Henry asked.

The kid backpedaled a few steps. "Parker.

Ask her." He gestured to Riley. "We're in the same anthropology class."

Henry turned his gaze on Riley. She nodded but kept her lips clamped together. Not sure why his sister was so freaked out, Henry regarded Parker.

The kid looked like he'd skipped too many meals. Slim with baggie jeans and a T-shirt that hung on his long-limbed frame. His dark hair needed some attention. The kid looked vaguely familiar, but Henry couldn't place where he'd seen him.

"Well, you best get on with your assignment then," Henry said. "Let Riley do hers."

The kid shrugged and sauntered away, disappearing into another exhibit.

Riley hiked her backpack higher on her shoulder. "I had it handled."

Sure didn't look that way to Henry. "What did he want?"

"Nothing." Riley stepped around him and trotted off to join her friends.

"That didn't look like nothing," Henry muttered. He didn't like that Riley was keeping secrets. A warm, soft hand on his arm drew his attention to Olivia.

"She might open up to me," she said.

He stared at her for a long moment. "You could be right. She likes you. Maybe later, you can take a run at her. Unless, of course, you think that's too smothering of me."

"Not smothering at all. Just a concerned big brother." She patted his arm before stepping away. "If you'll excuse me, I'm going to the ladies' room."

Henry watched her walk away, torn between the need to escort her and keep Riley in sight. Olivia was an officer of the law and could take care of herself. He and Cody hurried to find his sister.

Olivia checked her reflection in the restroom mirror one last time. Her baby bump was a bit more pronounced today. And she was feeling a bit queasy for other reasons. Like the way she'd let her guard down around Henry. She couldn't deny how nice it was to relate to him in a friendly manner. But she would have to remember to keep up the emotional barrier that her job demanded or there would be a steep cost. One she wasn't sure she was ready to pay.

Adjusting her purse over her belly, she stepped into the hall. Rough hands grabbed her from behind and pushed her up against the wall, knocking the breath from her lungs.

Panic for her unborn child speared through her. She was thankful her purse provided a cushion of sorts against the hard wall.

An arm pressed against the back of her neck and a hand pressed on the middle of her back, holding her in place.

A male voice spoke close to her ear. "It's not fair. You better find him guilty of hurting Davey Carrell or someone else is going to get hurt."

SIX

This wasn't a drill. Olivia had been trained by the best. She knew what to do when attacked from behind. Though her blood pounded in her ears and panic threatened to render her immobile, Olivia focused despite the adrenaline spike and gripped her right fist with her left hand. Using momentum and exerting every ounce of strength she possessed in both arms, she rammed her right elbow into her assailant's gut. He let out a loud groan.

Not satisfied with her effort, she followed her defense tactic with a hard heel stomp on his instep. The assailant cursed, released his hold and danced back. Olivia spun in time to see his retreating back and head covered by a dark hoodie. The guy pulled the fire alarm before he rounded the corner and disappeared from sight.

Covering her ears with her hands against the loud shriek of the alarm bouncing off the walls, Olivia gave pursuit, but there was no sign of the hooded figure among the now-panicked crowd rushing toward the exit. He'd escaped.

She had to find Henry and Riley.

Stepping out of the path of a woman dragging her school-age son toward the exit, Olivia grabbed her phone from her purse and shot off a text to Henry, telling him to meet her at the West 77th Street exit.

Within moments, Henry, Cody and Riley hurried toward her, dodging through the crush of people intent on vacating the museum.

"Are you okay?" he asked, his hand touching her elbow in a comforting way that rendered her speechless for a second.

Riley's eyes were huge with fear. "The museum is on fire!"

Regaining her wits, Olivia shook her head. "No, it's not." She told them what happened.

"What?" Henry put his hand on her shoulder. "Did he injure you?"

With a gasp, Riley clutched at Olivia. "You were assaulted? In the museum?"

"I'm fine," Olivia assured the siblings. "He threatened that someone would get hurt if I don't find you guilty of the charges."

"Can you ID him?" Henry's hands clenched and his gaze scanned the area.

"I didn't get a look at his face. He pulled the alarm and ran off. I looked for him, but he'd escaped."

Riley shivered. "That's scary."

Anger flashed in Henry's dark eyes. "We have to talk to security. They'll have video footage. Maybe we can identify the guy and see where he went."

All around them, people, mostly tourists, hurried toward the exits. The elevators were left open. People flooded down the staircases from the upper floors toward the doors leading out of the building.

Henry led the way through the crowd to the security offices near the ground level entrance in the Theodore Roosevelt Memorial Hall.

"Sir, you and your party need to exit." A guard stopped them and pointed to the nearest doors leading to the street.

Henry reached into his pocket and flashed his badge at the man. "There's no fire." He explained the situation. "I need to speak to the person in charge."

The guard shook his head. "I have to follow protocol. Everyone out until the fire department makes the determination that it's safe."

Riley tugged on Henry's arm. "Please, let's just go." The young girl grabbed Olivia's arm. "Come on."

Sensing the depth of Riley's distress, Olivia said to Henry, "You can check the video footage later. We should get your sister out of here."

Henry took a breath then nodded. "Yes. Though you'll need to give a statement about the assault."

Heart thumping in her chest, she said, "I will. But not here."

They hurried through the exit door and out on to Central Park West. Seeking shelter in the shade of a tree as a fire engine came to a halt at the curb in front of them, they watched as firefighters in turnout uniforms spilled out.

Two uniformed officers approached and took Olivia's statement.

"Stay here," Henry said. "I'm going to talk to the fire chief." He and Cody hurried away.

Riley moved closer to Olivia. "I don't like this. We need to go home."

Olivia slipped her arm around Riley. "Don't worry. Your brother won't let anything happen to you."

"But who's going to protect Henry?" Riley asked. "Someone's out to get him."

Olivia's gaze sought out the man in question. There was no refuting the girl's words. Someone wanted to take Henry down. And were willing to hurt other people to make it happen. Why?

A wave of protectiveness coursed through her. She would do what she could for Henry.

But she also had a job to do. She'd have to write up a report about the threat and explain her reasoning for being with Henry and Riley at the museum. She hoped her boss would see the value of spending time with Henry outside of the department atmosphere. She was gaining a better understanding of him as a man, which would be incorporated into her assessment for the review board. And though she prayed she'd be able to prove him innocent, she couldn't get emotionally involved, no matter the outcome. Unfortunately, doing as she should was proving harder with every moment she spent in Henry's presence.

Henry kept an eye on his sister and Olivia where they stood together under the shade of a large tree. His heart pounded in his chest like a runaway subway train. He'd known the moment he caught sight of Olivia hustling back from the restroom that something had been wrong. Her eyes were large and her pupils dilated.

Agitation revved through his system. He

wished he'd been there to catch Olivia's assailant in the act. Unfortunately no one close to him was safe while he was being targeted.

Even now, he didn't like being very far away from either of the women. He told himself he was doing his job where Olivia was concerned. But honestly, he couldn't say there was any discernible difference between the fear he experienced for Olivia's safety than the fear he had for Riley's safety. It didn't matter that Olivia was a trained officer who had proven moments ago that she was more than capable of taking care of herself. He couldn't curb the protective instinct any more than he could keep from breathing. He was coming to care for this woman, despite knowing he shouldn't if he valued his career.

He shook off his thoughts and forced his mind to focus on what was happening around him. People continued to stream out of the museum. Cody's head swiveled in an arc, his nose in the air but still no sign of alarm.

Henry searched for anyone matching the description that Olivia had given of the hooded man. If only she had seen his face, rather than just his back as he'd run away. He could've ditched the hoodie at any time. The guy could be watching them now.

This had to be the same man who'd tried to break into the condo. Especially hearing that the assailant insisted Olivia find him guilty in her investigation. Henry needed to question Davey Carrell and find out which of his friends would be bold enough to act with such malicious intent.

Unfortunately, Henry couldn't go near Davey.

For now, the best thing that Henry could do was take his sister and Olivia as far away from this area as possible. He would call his sergeant and request that someone question Davey.

After talking to the fire chief and touching base with the head security guard to request he send any relevant video to the K-9 Unit's tech, Henry ushered Olivia and Riley back to Brooklyn. They took a cab rather than the subway.

The cab bounced along the road with the three of them squished in the back seat and Cody on his lap. Riley sat in the center and snuggled up against him.

"Did you get enough material for you to complete your assignment?" Olivia asked Riley.

"I did," she answered with a shudder. "I'm really glad you both were with me." She nudged him with her elbow. "We should have a barbecue," she said. "Invite Olivia and maybe the McGregors and the Jamesons."

He was glad Riley liked his colleagues. "Soon. But not today. I think adding anyone else into the mix right now would be unwise. I'm being targeted and those around me apparently are, as well." His stomach clenched with dread.

It was no coincidence that Riley had been at Coney Island when the bomber reached out to Henry. And now Olivia had been attacked. He didn't want to draw anyone else into the line of fire.

Olivia turned to look at him, her gaze intense, and then she said to Riley, "It's very sweet of you to want to include me. But I really need to get home. My kitty has probably clawed her way through the door of the pantry trying to get to her food."

Riley's eyes grew big and she clapped her hands. "You have a kitty? I love kittens. Henry won't have one with Cody around."

Olivia's gaze jumped to Henry, then Cody. "Cody doesn't get along with cats?"

Henry shrugged. "I don't know. We've never encountered one up close."

"Henry doesn't like cats," Riley said.

He met Olivia's gaze. "It's not that I dislike them so much as never been around them."

"Can we come to your house and see your kitten?" Riley asked.

"She's not a kitten," Olivia said. "But I'm sure Kitty would appreciate a little love and attention."

"You named your cat Kitty?" Henry asked.

Olivia's nose twitched. "She's two years old, I think. She adopted me a few months ago. Just showed up at the apartment complex one day and wouldn't let anyone else near her but me. I tried to find her owners, because she's a unique type of cat, but no one claimed her. And yes, I named her Kitty because I could never decide on anything better."

"She adopted you?" Riley clapped her hands together. "That's so sweet."

When they reached Olivia's building and she led them inside, Henry was surprised by the small one-bedroom apartment. He'd wasn't sure what he'd expected, maybe more of a minimalist sort of vibe, but instead the place was very artsy with lots of personality.

Her walls were covered with paintings of beautiful landscapes and there were sculpted pieces on every available space. The blue suede couch and red and white accent chair invited one to sit down for a cozy chat.

One corner of her living room was devoted to crafting, with a table and bins filled with all sorts of materials he recognized because Riley was also into crafting. Though Riley didn't keep her supplies as neat and organized as Olivia. This was a different side to the lieutenant and reminded him that she was an attractive woman with depth. In other circumstances, he'd want to explore the many layers she possessed. But he couldn't. And wouldn't.

"Here Kitty, Kitty," Olivia called.

From the bedroom they heard a soft meow. Cody's ears perked up and he cocked his head, listening. How would the dog react when confronted with a cat in close quarters?

"Can I go get her?" Riley asked.

"Hold on a sec." Olivia dug into a box of treats and handed several pieces to Riley. "She may be hiding under the bed. She's really sweet. But just be cautious because she doesn't know you."

Concern arced through Henry. "Maybe she shouldn't be handling a cat that doesn't know her."

"I'll be fine," Riley said. "I know how to handle animals."

Olivia stayed Riley with a hand. "Your brother's right. It might be better for me to bring her out." She hurried down the hall, disappearing into her bedroom.

Riley whirled on him. "Really? Now the cat's unsafe?"

"You heard Olivia, she doesn't know if how the cat will respond to you."

Riley rolled her eyes and walked over to the crafting corner. He blew out a breath. There didn't seem to be any winning with his sister. Her phone chimed. She looked at the text, her mouth pulling at the corners.

"Everything okay?" Henry asked.

With another roll of her eyes, she put her phone away. "Yes."

Henry had the urge to stick out his tongue at her. That would be acting just as childishly as her, but sometimes she brought out his inner twelve-year-old.

A few moments later, Olivia arrived back into the living room carrying the strangest creature Henry had ever seen. "What is *that*?"

Cody lifted his nose toward the animal in question, sniffed, then lost interest. He settled down at Henry's feet.

"A sphynx, or Egyptian hairless cat," Olivia said. "Though they aren't really hairless. Their skin is covered with a fine layer of down. Like a peach." She held the cat out. "Pet her."

He'd never seen a cat of this breed in real life. Its pink skin was wrinkled, its ears too big for its head and the cat's piercing blue eyes stared at him, unblinking.

"She looks like E.T.'s cousin." But he had to admit, as he ran his hand over her back, that her suede-like coat was velvety soft.

Riley stepped up and held out the treat Olivia had given her earlier. Very daintily, Kitty took the treat from Riley's fingers. Then she clawed the air as if trying to gain traction so she could get into Riley's arms. Olivia handed the cat over. Riley hugged Kitty to her chest, petting and cooing. Soon a loud rumble of purring filled the air.

"She likes you, Riley," Olivia said. "Can I get either of you something to drink?"

"No, thank you," Henry said. "We should get going."

Riley spun away and walked back to the crafting table with Kitty in her arms. "You're a crafter. What are you working on over here?"

Olivia joined Riley in the craft corner. Henry stood back, his heart aching as he realized that Riley was becoming attached to Olivia. No doubt Riley was starved for maternal attention.

The two women talked about mosaic glass and art. He had to admit he respected and admired the Internal Affairs investigator. And he was attracted to her. None of that was good.

Olivia would be a good influence on his little sister, but it wasn't a good idea for him and Olivia to be spending time together. Riley shouldn't form a bond with the woman.

He had to distance himself. Not only for

Olivia's safety but also because his life, his career, was on the line.

He would walk a tightrope from the Chrysler Building to the Empire State Building if it meant he could continue doing the job he loved.

Long after Henry, Cody and Riley left, Olivia sat on the couch staring out the window and watching the sun set. Kitty sat curled on her lap. Every time her child moved, she was reminded of the life growing inside of her and it filled her with tender love. All in all, it had been a good day. Up to the point where she'd been assaulted outside the ladies' restroom.

But even before the assault, Henry had been attentive and caring. A true gentleman.

How was she going to find it within herself not to become emotionally involved in this case?

They drilled it into her at the academy that an Internal Affairs investigator was to stay neutral, unbiased and unemotional and she was struggling. Did it mean she wasn't cut out for this job? Or that her heart really wasn't in it? She suspected the latter. And not just because of Henry and her growing feelings for him.

She could still vividly remember her hesitation when she took the position with IA. But her family had cheered her on. Even Roger had been supportive, a rare moment for him. She'd accepted the post and had spent the first six months shadowing another investigator. If her family hadn't pushed her toward the career she wasn't sure she'd have applied. But she did find the fact finding, interviewing and presentation of cases for the review board came easily. Her father had been so proud of her when she'd made the transfer to internal affairs.

She couldn't let him or the department down.

"I can handle this," she said aloud. "I'm a professional. I can do my job and keep my emotions in check."

But was that what she wanted? And what would be best for her baby? The questions ricocheted through her mind as the night went on.

In the morning, instead of heading to her family's congregation, she took the subway to the church near Henry and Riley's house.

Yesterday Riley had mentioned where they attended services and had asked Olivia to accompany them. Telling herself she was only trying to get a better understanding of Henry and his life, she had told Riley she would think about it. She'd thought of nothing else all night.

Now here she was, walking up the concrete steps to the big arched doorway. What if Henry and Riley didn't show up today?

The thought should have brought her some relief, but it didn't. She grew more agitated as she stepped inside the doors. A sea of unfamiliar faces lay before her in the pews. What was she doing here? She should be with her family not...not what? Chasing after Henry?

No. She certainly wasn't chasing anyone. On the verge of turning around and leaving, she heard Riley call her name.

Riley waved from a pew near the front. Olivia's gaze jumped from Riley to Henry, who remained seated but had twisted toward her. For a moment, their gazes locked, his showing surprise. Then his mouth curved upward and he gave her a nod as if also inviting her to join them. Her heart did a funny little skip that left her breathless.

Drawn forward by some invisible tether, she could hear people whispering and sense the gaze of everyone in the church. Did these people know she was crossing a line?

Feeling conspicuous, she slid into the pew. Riley hugged her, then scooted around her so that now Olivia was wedged between the siblings. Cody, wearing his K-9 vest, lay at Henry's feet. The dog nudged her foot with his nose.

Henry leaned close. "This is unexpected."

Her defensiveness rose. "Riley invited me."

Riley's smile was wide. "I did invite her." She glanced away and then waved to someone. "There's my friend Nicole. I'll be right back." She shimmied out of the pew and down the middle aisle, leaving Olivia and Henry alone on the bench.

"Are you on duty?"

"Not officially," Henry said, his voice low. "But my sergeant suggested I keep Cody close until we catch the bomber. We walked the perimeter before we sat down."

"Makes sense." Though Olivia hated to think something could happen here in this sacred place, having Cody's super nose around to interpret any dangerous odors would keep everyone safe.

The clearing of a throat behind them drew Henry's attention. Olivia followed his gaze. An older couple with big grins regarded her with obvious curiosity.

"Larry and Martha Hodgeson, this is Olivia Vance. A friend," Henry said.

Surprise jumped inside of Olivia at Henry's statement. Did he consider her a friend? Were they friends? *Could* they be friends? She liked the idea way more than she should. She swallowed the trepidation of fraternizing with Henry that threatened to rob her of the moment.

Extending his hand, Larry said, "Hello, Olivia. Welcome."

Olivia shook the offered hand, appreciating the man's sincerity. "Thank you."

Martha sat forward, her brown eyes twinkling in her gently lined face. "How do you two know each other?"

"Work," Henry stated and pointed toward the lectern. "Services are about to start."

He faced forward. Sharing his apparent discomfort at the pointed question, Olivia pressed her lips together, smiled and faced the front of the church. Henry leaned close and whispered in her ear. "I wish everybody would mind their own business."

She glanced at him, not realizing he'd turned back toward her. Their lips nearly touched. Her gaze bounced from the wonderful shape of his mouth to his gaze. What she saw there made her heart pound.

"I should leave," she whispered. And regain her senses.

"Please don't. I'm glad you're here."

His words uncurled a ribbon of joy inside her. It had been so long since anyone had made her feel wanted and special. She was in so much trouble. Straightening her spine, she reminded herself she had to keep things between them professional. She was here to gather more intel on what Henry was like off duty—or rather, away from the station house—so she could make a more informed judgment on his character and conduct. Both of which were proving to be stellar.

The sermon started and Riley never returned but had decided to remain farther back in the sanctuary with her friends.

Olivia struggled to track the pastor's message. But finally the words penetrated through her distraction with stinging clarity. "Forgive those who have wronged you so that you may be forgiven." Her thoughts turned to her late husband.

Emotions clogged her chest, an ugly mix of anger, betrayal and grief. She wanted to forgive him but she didn't know how. The hurt was still so close to the surface. And every time she tried to let go, she only ended up with a headache.

"You okay?"

She didn't want Henry to see the ugliness inside of her. Shoring up her defenses, she smoothed away her inner turmoil and nodded.

When the pastor had finished his sermon, Riley returned. Riley leaned over to talk to Henry, practically pushing Olivia into his side. He was solid and warm against her and she was hard-pressed to not melt into him.

"Can Nicole come over?" Riley asked.

Henry nodded. "Of course."

With a satisfied smile, Riley sat back. "Good. Maybe the four of us could go to brunch at The Pancake House."

Oh, Olivia was so tempted to say yes. Brunch sounded lovely and was her favorite meal of the day. She had promised herself she wasn't going to become emotionally involved with these people and yet, here they were, like a family, on the brink of going out to brunch on Sunday after church. The line between professional and personal was blurring. Somehow she had to make that line more defined.

Heaviness descended on her shoulders as longing for a complete family of her own wrapped around her like a wet blanket. She pushed it away. Soon she would have her own child to lavish with the love in her heart. And no matter how much she was attracted to Henry or how much she adored Riley, she was afraid to trust, to risk her heart again.

Riley was an adult, ready to launch herself into the stratosphere of her life. And Henry had already made it clear he wasn't interested in raising a family after raising his sister. All good reasons for Olivia to be putting the brakes on whatever it was she was feeling. Her job required her to erect an emotional barricade. Plus, after her late husband's betrayal, how could she trust again? Being suddenly reminded of her disastrous marriage served as a wake-up call. Best to guard her heart to keep from being hurt in the future.

Abruptly, Olivia stood, shaking her head. "I'm sorry, you two. I need to head home for Kitty. And then I've got a full day of—stuff to do. Errands."

She shuffled past Riley into the aisle.

"Olivia?" Henry's concerned voice followed her.

She waved and headed out the door at a fast clip, dodging people as she went, smiling apologetically instead of stopping when she realized that many in the congregation wanted her to pause so they could grill her about who she was and why she was with Henry and Riley.

She hurried out to the crosswalk. The light turned green for her to cross and she stepped into the street, heading toward the subway station.

A silver sedan pulled away from the curb, its tires squealing on the pavement drawing her attention. The car was speeding straight at her.

SEVEN

Strong hands wrapped around Olivia's biceps and yanked her backward out of the car's path, up against a hard chest. The sedan shot past her so closely the air swirled in the late morning heat. The car made a sharp left, taking the corner at the end of the street with a screech of rubber gripping the road and disappeared out of sight. The license plate was conspicuously missing.

Shock and adrenaline coursed through Olivia's veins, making her limbs shake.

Henry slipped his arms around her, holding on to her as her knees buckled. "I've got you."

His deep voice reverberated through her and she twisted in his arms to look at him. "That car—" Her voice faltered.

"—Almost ran you down." The sharp edge of his anger sliced the air between them.

"You saved me." Gratitude engulfed her along with a good dose of affection. If he hadn't followed her out...

His expression softened, his mouth tipping up at one corner in a crooked smile that snuck into her heart and gave it a squeeze.

"Are you okay?"

Suddenly aware that Henry was holding her like a man would a woman he loved and that she wanted nothing more than to lean forward and kiss him, she gasped and wiggled out of his arms. The sting of a blush heated her cheeks. She hoped Henry didn't notice. "Thank you, Henry."

He stuffed his hands into his pockets. "No problem."

"I called 911," a man from the church said.

"We appreciate your help," Henry told the man.

Olivia took a step toward the sidewalk and nearly stumbled over the curb. Henry slid an arm around her waist to steady her. Then he tucked her hand around his arm. "Riley and I will see you home as soon as we've given our statements to the first responders."

"You don't—"

"Olivia, let us do this for you."

She was shaky, and at the moment, being alone was really the last thing she wanted. She prayed that this little jolt of adrenaline hadn't hurt the baby. She'd read that that could happen. She made a mental note to call her ob-gyn on Monday.

Henry stared at her, his gaze intense. "Are you sure you're all right? I mean, considering—"

She held up a hand, stopping him from finishing his sentence. "I'm fine. *Everything* is fine. Okay?"

He may suspect she was pregnant, but she did not want to discuss her baby with the man she was investigating. If anyone found out that she'd opened up about something so personal, she might as well just turn in her badge now. And that wasn't going to happen. If, or when, she resigned from the police force, it would be her decision. She was done allowing herself to be pressured into circumstances and situations she didn't fully embrace.

Seeming to accept her pronouncement, Henry nodded. "Good." He beckoned for Riley. As they waited for the young woman and her friend to join them, Henry said, "This wasn't an accident."

Olivia shivered, wishing she was still ensconced in his embrace. "I realize that. You said you'd thought a silver sedan was following you the other night?"

His dark eyes hardened. "I did. And I'm pretty sure that was the same car. Did you get a look at the driver?"

She shook her head. All she'd seen was sunlight reflecting off the grill as the sedan sped forward, aimed in her direction. "You?"

"Not enough for a description. He had on sunglasses and the visor was down. He had black gloves and a hoodie on just like the guy who tried to break into my condo."

"Do you think this is the same guy who assaulted me yesterday at the museum?"

"We have to assume so," he said.

Which meant the man targeting Henry and those close to him was growing impatient. But what was his endgame? If his goal was to hurt Henry, why go after her when she was the only one who could ruin Henry's career?

Monday morning, Henry stopped at Eden's desk with coffee cups in both hands. He set one in front of the tech guru.

Eden glanced between the cup and him. "This is for me?"

"I didn't want you to think I was ungrateful for all the work you do."

She smiled at him, her dark eyes twinkling as she reached down to pet Cody. "Hey, handsome." She picked up the coffee and took a sip. "Hmm. Perfect. How did you know the way I take my cup of joe?"

He grinned. "A wise man takes notice of what a person wants when asking her for a favor."

"Well, I'm glad I don't have to disappoint you today." She swung around to her monitors. Her fingers flew across the keyboard.

"So I pulled up all the video footage from the surrounding area where the bomb went off in Coney Island. As well as around Joey Yums, like you asked."

She pressed Enter and the video monitors lit up. The far monitor showed a perfect shot of the front of the Joey Yums restaurant. The middle monitor had a street view in front of the eatery and the third monitor showed a long shot of the boardwalk.

The time stamp on the video was from a half hour before Henry had arrived. Eden hit the fast-forward button.

"Wait!" Henry sucked in a sharp breath. Eden stopped the video on a clear shot of Riley and her friends entering Joey Yums. Five minutes later, they exited with food containers that they ate from while walking along the boardwalk, passing very close to the garbage can that later exploded. Henry's heart rate doubled. It was one thing to suspect how close his sister had come to disaster and another to see it in color.

As soon as Riley and her friends walked out of the view on the third monitor, a hooded figure wearing a backpack could be seen from the direction of the street. The guy kept his face averted as if he knew where the cameras were located. Sunlight glinted off the guy's sunglasses. He walked toward Joey Yums's entrance before doing an about-face and walking slowly down the boardwalk in the same direction as Riley and her friends.

The guy walked past the last garbage bin and disappeared off screen. Henry frowned. "He's clearly following Riley, but he's not our bomber."

Eden held up a hand. "Wait for it."

A minute later the hooded figure returned, his body angled so the camera couldn't record his face, but he seemed to be staring at the young couple kissing on the bench. Then the guy took off the backpack, lifted the lid of the garbage can and dropped the backpack inside. He shut the lid and jogged away. The couple on the bench didn't appear to even notice him. They were too entwined in each other's arms to realize that disaster was right next to them.

"I want to see this bomber again."

Eden rewound the video.

Henry studied what he could see of the man. Jeans, tennis shoes and the edges of dark sunglasses, but Henry couldn't determine the man's race. But he did notice the black gloves on the bomber's hands, just like the ones worn by the prowler at the condo and the driver of the sedan. "This has to be the same guy who tried to run down Lieutenant Vance."

Eden turned to stare at him. "What?"

He told her about the incident at the church and the museum.

"Oh, that's why the museum called," Eden said. "I haven't had a chance to return the call, but I will. In the meantime, let me see if I can find any video footage around the church for you."

He told her the approximate time and the make and model of the car. He pointed to the screen where the hooded figure stood frozen on the boardwalk. "Can you backtrack this guy's route on the street? See where he came from?"

"I can," she said. "But it will take some time. I can text you when I have something more to show you."

"That'd be great. Any chance you have any information on the phone that was used to contact me?"

"Sorry, it was a burner phone. It's turned off now. But I have a program running to alert me if it turns back on."

Henry wasn't surprised that the phone was a dead end, but he couldn't stop the wave of frustration and helpless anger roaring through him.

Eden waved at him. "I don't like when people stand over my shoulder. Why don't you go to the unit meeting? I'll text Gavin that I'm still working."

"Thanks," Henry said. "I owe you one." He seemed to owe a lot of people these days. Even his boss, Gavin, who'd promised to send someone to talk to Davey Carrell about which of his friends might be threatening Henry and those close to him.

Eden turned back to her screen as if he hadn't spoken.

Henry and Cody headed downstairs to the conference room where the meeting was taking place. Gavin was at the front of the room getting ready to call the meeting to order.

Henry and Cody slipped inside and took up a spot against the back wall.

A minute later, Olivia stepped inside the room and took a place next to him. Surprise washed over him. It wasn't usual for IA to attend a precinct meeting, but considering the encompassing nature of her investigation, he supposed observing the unit as a whole, and him specifically, wasn't out of line. Their gazes locked for a moment. He was stunned to see the flare of interest in her amber eyes before she quickly turned her gaze forward. She looked good this morning, as regal as she had on Friday, but today's suit color was a deep purple with a striped, collared shirt underneath. Her hair was in a fancy braided updo. His blood surged with a confusing mix of attraction and affection.

When he'd dropped her off at her apartment yesterday after her near-disaster with the sedan, he'd been hard-pressed to leave her alone. Only her assurance that she'd planned on staying inside for the rest of the day until one of her brothers arrived to take her to their parent's house for dinner had relieved some of his anxiousness.

He had to admit he was glad to see her this morning unharmed. He'd hate it if something happened to her because of him. The need to protect her rose strong within him. He fought the urge to put an arm around her. She would probably deck him. And he'd deserve it.

"I have an announcement everyone," Gavin said from the front of the room, drawing Henry's and the whole room's attention. All the officers went silent. "Thanks to US Marshal Emmett Gage, who was able to grab a cup and napkin from Randall Gage, his cousin and our prime suspect in the McGregor murders, we have a DNA match."

The room erupted with cheers and gasps. K-9 Officer Belle Montera, who'd been assigned to question the US marshal about his cousin in the first place, seemed both relieved and subdued. Henry knew that Belle and Emmett Gage were engaged to be married, and to have absolute proof that his cousin *was* a murderer had to be tough on the dedicated law enforcement officer. Henry's gaze sought out his friend, Bradley McGregor, his heart gladdened by this new development. The long-unsolved murders of Bradley and Penny's parents had put a horrible strain on the siblings.

Bradley met his gaze. There were tears in his eyes as his arm slipped around his sister, seated beside him. Tears ran down Penny's face and she nearly collapsed sideways out of her chair.

"Okay, people," Gavin said, reclaiming everyone's focus. "We have our work cut out for us. Now we just have to find Randall, who hasn't been seen since he bolted from the greasy spoon weeks ago. The FBI and the US Marshals are on the trail. But we need to be vigilant. This man has killed two, possibly four, people. That we know of."

Henry knew the sergeant was referring to the recent double homicide of the Emerys, parents of a little girl who'd been left unharmed. The Emerys were killed on the twentieth anniversary of the McGregors' murders—with the same MO. Had Randall Gage also killed the Emerys? Or had that been the work of a copycat? The unit didn't know at this point, and it was frustrating. Henry glanced at K-9 Detective Nick Slater, who'd gotten personally involved with the aunt of little Lucy Emery—the lone survivor of her parents' murder—during the investigation. Nick and Willow were now in the process of formally adopting Lucy, and Henry could see from Nick's tight expression how bad he wanted justice for the Emerys.

"There wasn't any DNA found at the Emery crime scene, right?" Transit Officer Max Santelli asked. He stood near the window with his rottweiler at his side.

"Correct. There was no DNA evidence found on either of the victims. Or the evidence left behind. But our forensic expert is working hard on extracting DNA from fibers found on the back door knob of the Emory apartment."

"And if we can't match this evidence to Randall Gage?" Officer Jackson Davison asked. He sat at the conference table with his cadaver dog at his feet.

A grim look entered Gavin's eyes. "Then it's possible we have an entirely different killer on the loose. A copycat."

Henry's gut clenched with aggravation. He couldn't be on the case because of the charges being investigated by Internal Affairs. He swung his gaze to Olivia. She didn't look in his direction and kept her focus on Gavin.

Henry sent up a silent plea to God that Olivia would hurry up and finish her investigation. And find him innocent so he could get back to work and keep his family and friends safe. Including, the lovely IA lieutenant.

As Olivia stood at the back of the conference room, listening to Sergeant Sutherland's announcement of the DNA match and the possibility that the second murders might be a different killer, she had an idea. Hopefully she wouldn't be overstepping by sharing her thoughts with Gavin and his team.

She waved her hand to get Gavin's attention. Like everyone else in the city, she'd been following the double homicide case. Her conscience wouldn't keep her from speaking her mind.

Eyebrows rising, Gavin said, "Internal Affairs Lieutenant Olivia Vance has something she'd like to say."

All eyes turned to her. Heat infused her cheeks, but she straightened her spine and stepped forward. "If Randall Gage is the killer of both sets of parents, then he left *two* young children alive. He may view himself as a protector of children." A murmur of agreement swept through the room. "I would suggest two things. One, look for similar crimes where a child was spared. Two, contact the FBI's Behavioral Analysis Unit profiler, Caleb Black. He's the best of the best at Quantico."

Gavin studied her for a long moment. "Good ideas, both. We've considered the child-protector angle. I will reach out to the

FBI and see if they can spare Agent Black."
He turned back to his unit.

The dismissal was obvious. Slightly nauseous, Olivia stepped back into the shadow of the other unit officers. She could feel Henry's gaze like a laser on her, but she held her head high. She wouldn't apologize for speaking.

Gavin went on to report about other activity in the K-9 Unit. Twenty minutes later, when the meeting broke up, Olivia hightailed it out of the room as quickly as possible.

"Hey, Olivia, wait."

Henry's voice stopped her in the station's entryway. She really wanted to get some fresh air before she lost her breakfast all over the station's floor. Slowly, she turned and faced the man she was investigating.

Bracing herself to be told she'd crossed some imaginary line, she stiffened her spine and planted her feet apart, much like she'd seen her father and brothers do when faced with an adversary. Though calling Henry an adversary didn't sit well with her. Not after he'd saved her life yesterday. As well as how often she'd thought about kissing him. Would his lips be soft and giving or hard and demanding?

And what was that wonderful cologne that clung to his skin? She'd had to resist moving closer to him while they stood together at the unit meeting.

She really needed to get a grip. The influx of pregnancy hormones was messing with her head and her heart.

Henry strode to her side. His handsome face broke into a grin that set off a flutter in her tummy. She was pretty sure *that* wasn't the baby. She was helpless to curb the unprofessional attraction rooting inside of her.

"Good job on the suggestions," Henry said. "You really have a knack for reading situations and giving good advice."

His words were like a balm to her vulnerable state of embarrassment. "Thank you." She shrugged, trying to downplay the feeling of pride swelling within her chest. "I do have a degree in criminal justice as well as psychology."

His eyebrows rose. He rubbed a hand over

his now-shaven head. "Impressive. Why are you working in IA when you could be of more help as a counselor or even a criminal profiler for the NYPD or the FBI?"

His question stung. She had originally considered trauma counseling for victims, but that would have required deviating from family expectations. So she'd joined the police force, following in her father's and brothers' footsteps. She'd started out on patrol until her father had lectured her that the best way for her to earn respect and success was through Internal Affairs. Her father was a straight arrow who respected the difficult position of internal affairs and had stressed she had the goods to excel in IA.

Despite her best intentions, she'd let herself be pressured into a position she'd never really wanted, but her dad and brothers had convinced her she was a perfect fit for the job.

Now here was Henry questioning her choice of profession.

Was this some kind of tactic to get out of being investigated? She searched his dark gaze and found no hint of a hidden agenda.

Did she dare confess that she'd once considered a different path? Or that there were times when the isolation of Internal Affairs brought regret to the forefront of her mind?

Deciding that indulging in any personal give-and-take was too dangerous for her job and her peace of mind, she simply said, "I appreciate your thoughts. Now, if you'll excuse me, I have some old case files to go through." Better than confessing she was struggling with her attraction to him.

His mouth twisted in derision. "My old case files, no doubt."

Lying wasn't in her wheelhouse, so she nodded and couldn't stop the ache of regret that they were in this position. But the job was the job. No matter how distasteful she sometimes found it.

For a moment, he seemed to be wrestling with some inner turmoil and then he said, "Full disclosure, I had a previous claim leveled against me once in the early days of my career, but it was quickly ruled unsubstantiated."

Her heart sank. That didn't bode well for him. "Thank you for being up-front with me."

"Of course," he said. "I don't want there to be anything hidden between us."

Her heart gave a little jolt. She wasn't sure what to make of his statement, so she simply watched as he turned and strode away.

After taking a moment to splash water on her face in the restroom and doing some deep breathing exercises, she headed to the records room. An hour later, she found the case he'd referred to.

In looking at the date and knowing when Henry's father had died, there was no question Henry had been acting in grief during a domestic call where the wife was barely hanging on to life from a beating by her husband.

What Henry was doing on the job that day was a question she'd like answered by the department's psychologist, who'd deemed him fit for duty. But obviously the situation had triggered something in Henry, as when the male suspect had taken a swing at him, Henry had swung back.

Internal Affairs had cleared Henry of wrongdoing.

But still, the knowledge that Henry had reacted out of anger and grief was something she needed to take into account and address with him. To be fair, she wanted to hear his side of the story so she could understand his thought process at the time. And it might help her to discern what happened the night that Davey Carrell was injured.

After asking around for Henry's location, she found him in the training center next door to the precinct.

She entered a warehouse-size room filled with an eclectic mix of obstacles. Luggage pieces of various shapes and sizes were stacked in three different groupings. There was a bicycle rack with several bicycles locked up. A shrink-wrapped stack of pallets and a car-shaped cutout caught her eye. Plus multiple boxes of various shapes and sizes were intermittently scattered between all the other obstacles.

Stepping into an alcove where she could observe Henry and Cody moving through the obstacles without distracting them, Olivia watched in fascination as the beagle sniffed along the seams of the luggage, the edges of the boxes and around the pallets and would either move along or stop and sit.

A petite blonde wearing the training center uniform would clap when Cody sat, prompting Henry to pull out a toy from his pocket and play tug with Cody for a moment before resuming their activity. Olivia inferred that meant Cody had detected correctly.

Henry glanced up and met her gaze. His eyebrows lifted, then a slow smile curved his mouth as if he were pleased to see her again. An answering pleasure wound through her, making her heart thump with a yearning that made her knees wobbly.

It had been a mistake to search him out when she didn't have her emotions under control. But there was something about Henry, his vitality and his integrity, that called to her.

And made doing her job that much more difficult.

EIGHT

On the verge of retreating from the training center in a flood of embarrassment at her silly response to Henry, Olivia backed up and ran smack into the veterinarian, Gina.

Gina had Maverick, the runt of Brooke's litter, in her arms. Brooke was the sweet German shepherd a few of the K-9 officers had rescued from the streets soon after she'd given birth to five puppies. "Good morning."

"Morning." Olivia reached out to pet the pup. Gina handed him over. Olivia fumbled to hang on to the little dog. "Oh, okay."

"He responds well to you," Gina said.

Snuggling the dog close, Olivia's heart melted. She liked the sweet little guy. "Do you think one day he'll be able to train like Cody?"

"Too soon to know yet," Gina said. "Some dogs you can tell right away and in others it takes a little time to discern what kind of training, if any, they will be able to handle."

"What Cody's doing is very specialized, correct?"

"It is. Though there are now more bomb-sniffing dogs being trained all over the country than ever before," Gina replied. "Cody is checking for chemical vapors that come off the materials of the different obstacles, searching for specific odors that indicate evidence of an explosive device."

"Vapors? I didn't realize bombs had vapors." Olivia remembered the way the beagle had behaved at the boardwalk on Coney Island. "But that makes total sense with the way that Cody had sniffed the air and followed a scent to the garbage can that did explode."

Gina nodded. "Precisely. Everything gives off an odor. Cody has been trained to deconstruct each scent into its components, picking up on the chemicals he has been trained to detect. Kind of like when you step into an Italian restaurant and you smell that delicious aroma of spaghetti sauce. We know what goes into the sauce, but our noses can't differentiate between the tomatoes, garlic, rosemary, onion and oregano. But the dog can."

"That's amazing." Olivia cocked her head as she watched the way Henry was tracing the car outline with his hand and Cody's nose followed. "What are they doing now?"

"Henry is teaching Cody where he wants him to smell."

When the pair were done and heading out of the training ring, Olivia handed Maverick back to Gina. "Thank you for letting me hold him again."

"Anytime." Gina carried the pup away.

There was something so soothing about cuddling with Maverick. Feeling calmer and more like herself, Olivia hurried to catch up to Henry and Cody. They were walking toward the men's changing room.

Acutely aware of the other officers and trainers in the area, she called, "Detective

Roarke," stopping him in his tracks. "Could I have a moment of your time?"

His gaze bounced to the file folder in her hand, then back to her eyes. "It will have to be after I'm done in the training ring."

"You and Cody aren't done?"

"Not exactly." He handed her Cody's leash. "Hang on to him for a moment, will you?"

Without waiting for a reply, he opened the men's room door and disappeared inside.

Sputtering, she had half a mind to follow him inside and tell him she was not his lackey. Not that she minded hanging out with Cody, but still. But Henry wasn't one of her brothers, who she could boss around.

At last night's family dinner, her older brothers had given her a hard time for having jammed up their friend. She hated that she had to defend herself, especially when she wouldn't be in this position if not for their urging. She didn't like being the bad guy everyone avoided. But having jammed up—police term for launching an official investigation—Henry was her job.

A job that was becoming more than she could tolerate. Especially now that she was expecting a baby. The last thing she wanted was for her child to ever experience the sort of reserved animosity that was regularly flung her way.

Cody lay down at her feet, his paws on her shoe. There was no way she could be mad at the dog, at least. He was such a cutie with his floppy ears and masked face. His brown eyes regarded her with what she assumed was curiosity. The dog probably wondered why his handler had trusted her with him. She wondered the same thing and couldn't stop the spurt of pleasure crowding her chest.

Several long minutes later, Henry returned wearing a light-colored, padded bite suit and heavy boots. His head stuck out of the top, exposed, but in his hand, he carried a caged helmet.

Olivia chuckled and her earlier ire of having to cool her heels in the hallway dissipated. "You get to be the human chew toy."

Taking Cody's leash, he shot her a glance

and said wryly, "It would really help if you sped things along."

A brief stab of guilt provoked her to say, "I'm sorry, Henry, but my investigation will take however long it takes."

She really needed to do a thorough job that couldn't be questioned. Her integrity was at stake here in so many ways. She couldn't be rushed or bulldozed into making a determination, not by Henry, her family or some mysterious assailant. And certainly not her growing feelings for the handsome detective.

Henry and Cody walked ahead of her into the training ring, where K-9 Officer Lani Jameson, and her large German shepherd, Snapper, waited. Lani was dressed in her uniform and the dog had on a flak vest with the words K-9 Police emblazoned across the back.

Olivia followed the pair. "Is it normal for officers to wear full gear when training?"

Henry paused as if surprised to see her inside the arena. "Yes. Especially for the dog."

The K-9 trainer who'd been in the ring

earlier with Henry and Cody hurried over to take Cody's leash. "Who is that?" she whispered, nodding toward Olivia.

"Hi, Hannah," Henry said. "Olivia, this is Hannah O'Leary, one of the trainers and very protective of the center. Hannah, this is Lieutenant Olivia Vance of Internal Affairs."

Hannah's green eyes widened. Her mouth made a perfect *o*. "You definitely don't want to be in the ring for this, Lieutenant—for safety."

Frowning at the dire warning, Olivia moved out of the large circular arena to the spectator's area with Hannah and Cody.

"How's Snapper doing?" Olivia asked Hannah, eyeing the beautiful German shepherd who sat at attention in the ring next to Lani.

Last year the entire NYPD had been looking for Snapper, who'd gone missing after his handler and partner, Jordan Jameson, chief of the NYC K-9 Command Unit in Queens, was found murdered in a park. It had taken months for the dog to be reunited with the unit and Olivia had cheered along with everyone else when Snapper was found. When Lani transferred to the Brooklyn K-9 Unit, Snapper had been paired with her to keep the beloved police dog in the family, since Lani was married to one of Jordan's brothers, who'd become chief of the Queens unit. Olivia had seen pictures of the dog in the paper, but the images hadn't done the majestic shepherd justice. He looked fierce and capable of taking down an elephant, not at all cute like Cody.

Olivia held her breath as Henry put the caged mask on. Lani gave the thumbs-up sign, prompting Henry to run toward Lani and Snapper aggressively.

Lani unhooked Snapper's leash and gave the attack command. The dog was on Henry in a flash, his powerful jaws latching on to the padded arm of Henry's bite suit. Henry and the dog seemed to dance as Henry tried to shake the K-9 off. Lani gave another command and Snapper immediately released his hold on Henry's arm and hurried back to her side.

Olivia slapped a hand over her racing heart. She'd seen demonstrations of the K-9 officers, but it was different knowing the person in the bite suit. And realizing that the thick padding was the only thing keeping the dog's sharp teeth and powerful jaw from breaking Henry's skin or bones had her stomach knotting. They went through the exercise several times with Henry baiting the pair and then running away or grabbing at Lani. Each time, Snapper did his job and defended his K-9 handler with a ferociousness that was startling to observe.

Finally, Lani leashed up the panting shepherd and they headed out of the arena to a row of water bowls. Hannah opened the ring door to let Cody loose. The beagle raced across the ring then bit at Henry's padded ankles. Olivia turned to Hannah. "Is that normal for Cody?"

"All the dogs recognize the bite suit as training time," she replied.

Henry fell to the ground, his deep laughter echoing off the walls, as Cody's pink tongue darted in and out of the caged helmet's faceguard. That was the cutest thing Olivia had ever seen.

Hannah chuckled. "But obviously it's playtime for Cody."

Then another trainer brought out the pretty former-stray shepherd, Brooke, and her puppies, and let them loose in the arena. Henry slapped his hands on the matted floor and the puppies raced to his side, crawling over him and gnawing at him, their happy, yapping barks filling the room. The littlest puppy, Maverick, only made it a few feet before plopping down on his belly. The sight of the puppies with Henry was so cute Olivia took out her phone and snapped off several photos. She was sure Riley would appreciate the pictures.

Suddenly there was a cacophony of noise, as all of the dogs in the training center grew agitated. Barking and growling echoed off the walls and down the halls. The puppies' yipping turned to piercing panic. Cody howled like he was dying. Snapper and Brooke growled and barked aggressively at the air.

Unnerved by the sounds, Olivia covered her belly with her hand. "What's going on?"

"I don't know," Hannah answered. "But something's got the dogs spooked."

Just then, a red haze flowed out of the air ducts, filling the ring and the halls.

"It's some kind of gas!" Olivia shouted to be heard over the ruckus the dogs were making.

"Everyone out!" commanded Henry as he scooped up the puppies in one arm. Olivia darted out and picked up Maverick, holding him close to her chest. His little body shook uncontrollably.

Hannah raced to the kennel room along with Lani, Henry and Olivia not far behind, where they leashed up the dogs and ushered them all outside just as the fire alarms sounded.

"We have to be careful," Henry said at the exit. He handed the puppies off to the trainer. "This could be a ruse to get us out in the open."

Olivia's heart sank. "You think the bomber

will change tactics and start shooting? Or plant a bomb nearby?"

"Hard to say." Henry opened the door with caution. "Let me step out first."

Adjusting Maverick in her arms, Olivia met Lani's grim gaze. Henry could be stepping into the line of fire.

Please, Lord, keep him safe.

Henry stood in the open, slowly turning around as if baiting a sniper to take the shot. Then he was waving for Olivia and the others to leave the training center. Thankful to realize they wouldn't be picked off like the ducks in shooting gallery at Coney Island, she hurried outside.

Hannah set the puppies down on the grass. Henry quickly stripped out of his bite suit, leaving him in shorts and a K-9 unit T-shirt, before herding the active puppies, keeping them on the grass. Even Cody joined in, nudging a stray pup with his nose until the little dog turned around and headed away from the asphalt of the parking lot. The tender care Henry gave to the puppies and the other dogs made Olivia's insides turn to mush.

The ding of an incoming text chimed from Henry's pocket and made the hairs on Olivia's arm stand up. There was no reason for the dread suddenly stiffening her muscles with tension. Still, she hurried to his side and read the text along with him.

I can get you, anytime, anywhere.

Olivia couldn't believe what she was reading. "How did this maniac get to the air ducts?"

Henry's jaw worked. He shook his head. "I don't know. But I will find out."

She wanted to soothe away his upset over the disturbing text. But she didn't know how. The urgency to wrap up this case pressed down on her, but there were still so many questions she needed answered. It didn't help that the more time she spent with Henry, the more she was convinced he was truly a kind and caring man. The kind of man she once had hoped her own husband would be. The kind of man she wanted in her future.

She forced her thoughts away from what she couldn't change. Instead she focused on the fact that she was well on her way to caring for this handsome officer.

A fact that would most likely be her downfall.

Henry clutched his phone in a tight fist. Anger at the suspect for putting the dogs and everyone else in the training center at risk burned through him like a flare.

Olivia put her hand on his bare forearm. "No one was injured, and the dogs are safe as far as we can tell. The gas didn't seem to be toxic."

Taking comfort from her touch, he let some of the tension go. "Praise God for that."

"You acted quickly."

Her amber-colored eyes were soft and full of something that made it difficult to look away. "So did you."

Blinking, she turned away and squeezed

his arm. "There's the fire chief talking to Sergeant Sutherland."

Indeed, his boss and the chief were consulting. They needed to know about the text. Henry glanced around to see more officers had poured out of the K-9 unit and were now helping to corral the puppies and the working dogs.

He looked at Olivia. "Can you take charge of Cody?" The dog knew her and liked her. So did he. His stomach clenched. Had he lost his mind?

Her mouth curved. "Of course. Thank you for asking this time."

Grimacing, he said, "Sorry about that."

"You're forgiven."

Relief flooded him and loosened his muscles a little more. Thankfully she wasn't mad at him for his earlier heavy-handedness. Henry jogged over to the fire chief and Gavin and showed the two men the text.

The chief's eyebrows rose. "Not just a prank?"

"Prank?" Henry drew back, offended by the term. "This guy filled the whole training center with red smoke. Who knows what kind of damage that could have done."

"According to the fire chief, the gas was nontoxic," Gavin said. He scrubbed a hand over his face, his aggravation showing in his eyes.

"We found a couple of homemade smoke bombs in the air vents," the fire chief said. "When the air conditioning kicked on, it ignited them. They were made with a concoction of potassium nitrate, sugar and food coloring. Anyone with a computer could learn how to make one."

"We'll be sure to make those vents inaccessible going forward," Gavin said. "And look for other vulnerable areas around both the training center and the station house."

The chief nodded. "That would be wise."

For Henry, that the texting bomber hadn't wanted to hurt the dogs didn't excuse the panic the smoke had caused. Setting off the smoke bombs had been a warning to him, just as the text had been. He remembered the message delivered to Olivia in the museum. Her attacker had said she needed to find Henry guilty. "I really need to talk to Davey Carrell."

"You're not going anywhere near that young man," Gavin said. "Bradley and Tyler have interviewed him. He claims not to know who's harassing you."

Henry had full confidence that his friend and colleague Bradley along with Tyler Walker, another K-9 handler, had put pressure on Davey, but that didn't mean Davey had told them the truth. The kid was lying about his injuries. Unfortunately, Henry had no way to prove it.

"It's more than harassment, Sarge," Henry bit out. "Olivia was assaulted and almost run down. And Riley was too close to the boardwalk bomb for my comfort. Now this. A clear warning from the suspect."

Gavin stroked his chin. "I'm aware. As you requested, a patrol officer is keeping tabs on Riley. And as for Lieutenant Vance, her father has someone guarding her place at night and she's been instructed to stick close to the station while conducting her investigation. One of her brothers will be escorting her back and forth. However, you shouldn't be spending time with the lieutenant away from the station."

Henry was glad to hear precautions were in place to guard his sister and Olivia. And though he agreed keeping his distance from the attractive investigator was the best thing for them both, the thought didn't settle well in his gut. She'd already been targeted. The perpetrator had a bead on her. Henry doubted the perp would leave her alone just because Henry wasn't around her, which meant she was still vulnerable. Despite being a trained officer and fully capable of protecting herself, she was in danger because of him. He had to do what he could to mitigate the threat.

While the officers kept the dogs corralled, the fire department sucked all the smoke out of the training center fairly quickly and gave the all clear to return inside.

Once all the dogs were settled, Henry walked back to Olivia where she stood in the shade with Cody. "Okay, we can get back to your questions."

She stared at him, the unreadable expression in her eyes unnerving him. He usually could tell when she was irritated or amused. But now her emotions were shuttered from him. "Are you okay?"

She gave a nod. "But I need a breather. I'll have to catch up with you later. I do have some questions for you, but they can wait." She handed Cody's leash back to him and hurried away.

He wanted to call her back, but then decided he also needed a moment to decompress after the spike in adrenaline. After changing back into his uniform, he and Cody left the training center to find Eden. Hopefully she could trace the latest text he'd received.

Unfortunately, Eden confirmed this latest text also came from a burner phone that was untraceable. Frustrated with the lack of progress, Henry decided to check on Olivia. He discovered she'd left the station on foot. Alone.

Had she gone back to her apartment unaccompanied? Or somewhere close by? She'd been instructed to stay close to the station. He called her cell phone. She answered on the first ring.

"Henry? Is everything okay? Did something else happen?"

He appreciated that her first thought was the safety of others. "All good here. You left the station. I wanted to make sure you were all right."

There was a loud silence. Concern that he'd overstepped by admitting to worrying about her well-being, he grimaced but couldn't apologize.

"I'm fine," she finally said. "I'm at Sal's."

A measure of relief filled him. "Do you mind if I join you? For lunch. Nothing more."

"I suppose you have to eat, as well," she said, her tone wary.

"I'll be right there," he said and hung up.

With Cody at his side, Henry headed down the street at a fast clip. Normally he would leave his partner at the training center, but he wanted Cody's super nose available in case of trouble. And thankfully, Sal allowed the police dogs inside the pizzeria. His boss's warning to stay away from Olivia echoed in his head, but Henry had to put her safety ahead of what his boss wanted, even if it cost him everything. He refused to ponder why he was willing to risk it all for Olivia.

As he entered the eatery, the smell of garlic and tomato sauce filled Henry's nostrils and made his stomach rumble. But his gaze focused on the woman sitting at the corner table by the window. Olivia. Safe and sound, as she'd said.

The rush of relief and something else, something close to the sort of affection that made him very uncomfortable, rocked him back on his heels.

"Are you in line?" a woman holding a toddler asked.

"Uh, yes." He'd been caught staring but thankfully Olivia seemed oblivious to his presence. She stared into her salad as if the lettuce and veggies were the most engrossing thing ever.

He ordered a meat lover's special slice and

a small bowl of carrots for his partner before heading over to join Olivia while he waited for the order.

Cody nudged her knee, prompting her to scrub him behind his floppy ear. A smile tugged at the corners of her mouth and she made an obvious, yet valiant, effort to stop it.

He grinned and she sighed. That little noise did funny things to his insides.

Gesturing with her hand to the chair, she said, "Go ahead."

He turned the chair around and straddled it, facing her and stepped on Cody's leash. The dog lay on his belly, his head resting on his paws.

"You were supposed to be sticking close to the station house," Henry stated in a firm tone.

She lifted her chin and then surprise flared in her eyes. "You were worried."

"Yes." He had no problem admitting it. "I care what happens to you." Though that last bit took him by surprise, as well.

Her lips parted in a soft inhale, drawing his gaze to her mouth. Not for the first time, his breath quickened as attraction arced through him.

"I—" Olivia cleared her throat and glanced away as if to compose herself. She turned back to him, her expression contrite. "You're right. Leaving the K-9 unit alone wasn't the best decision I've made today."

He hadn't expected the humility or the appreciation crowding his chest. "I'm just glad you're okay."

For a moment she stared at him, her expression filled with wonder. Then she looked at her salad and stabbed a piece of lettuce with her fork.

"Roarke, order's ready."

Rising from the chair, he gave Cody the stay command with his hand and then he asked Olivia, "Can I get you anything while I'm up?"

"I'm good," she said. "I'm finishing my salad."

"No pizza today?" He remembered her appetite the last time they'd come to Sal's Pizzeria.

She smiled, her eyes brightening, making

him think she, too, remembered that night. "No, not today."

He went to the counter to pick up his slice. "Thanks, Sal."

"Isn't that the new IA investigator?"

Tension coiled in Henry's gut. "Yes. Lieutenant Vance."

Sal dropped his chin and stared at Henry with narrowed gray eyes. "Fraternizing with the enemy?"

NINE

Irritated by the retired officer's censure, Henry gritted his teeth and worked to calm his knee-jerk urge to reach across the space of the countertop and grab Sal by the apron strings. Sal wasn't wrong, after all.

Henry pulled in a deep breath and tried to keep his tone even. "Just eating, no fraternizing going on."

A voice in his head whispered, *Yeah, right*. He stubbornly ignored it.

Henry grabbed his food and stalked back to where Olivia was seated with Cody at her feet. He set the plate down with a clatter of ceramic on the red laminated tabletop.

Olivia and Cody jumped.

Olivia raised a dark eyebrow. "Everything okay?"

"Everything's dandy." He picked up his pizza and stuffed it in his mouth.

Just eating, no fraternizing going on.

There was a purpose to him being here with Olivia. Keeping her safe. And in the loop on what was happening. Not crushing on her. "I wanted to give you an update on the video feed from the boardwalk."

He proceeded to tell her what he'd seen on Eden's computer monitors while she pushed around her salad.

Olivia made a face. "So he was following Riley but didn't approach her and waited until she was out of the area before setting off his bomb."

"Looks that way."

"He didn't want to hurt her." Olivia's tone was thoughtful. "Do you think they could know each other?"

The bite of pizza soured in his stomach. The idea that his sister might be familiar with the texting bomber was unsettling. "I hope not."

He relayed what his boss had said about Davey Carrell. "And the burner phone used to text me has led nowhere. This guy seems to know how to cover his tracks."

"At least he was considerate enough not to put harmful smoke in the air ducts at the training center," she said. "The dogs are safe."

"Big consolation." He couldn't keep sarcasm from his voice. "It could have gone wrong if we hadn't been there to rush the dogs out."

"You were a hero today."

Her praise settled in his chest, making him feel like the hero she claimed him to be. He met her gaze. "We made an effective team. I couldn't have ushered all the puppies to safety without you."

She set down her fork. "That's not true. The others could have handled the situation without me, but I appreciate you saying it."

"It is true. I needed you today." He realized what he'd said and amended his words. "The dogs needed you."

"Sometimes it's good to be needed," she said, and her hand went to her stomach.

Henry sensed her mood shifting downward, no doubt to grief and sadness for her late husband. He reached across the table and covered her other hand before he even thought to stop himself. Her skin was warm beneath his. "You must miss him."

Her gaze jumped to his. "Who?"

Tucking in his chin, he said, "Your husband."

She jerked her hand from beneath his. "Yes, of course. He was my husband. Of course I miss him."

Her words rang hollow, as if she'd said them only to make him feel better.

"I heard the news report that he wasn't alone in the plane crash."

Her amber eyes glittered. For a second, he thought it may be tears but then he realized it was suppressed anger shining in her eyes. "That's correct."

His cop senses tingled, and he found himself searching his memory for details and pressing her. "They never identified who was in the plane, at least not publicly. Did you know who the other person was?"

"I'd never met her. But I've been told she was one of his dental hygienists."

"A work trip, then?" He hoped.

Her lips twisted. "Not unless booking a single suite in a romantic hotel on a private beach could be consider work-related."

Henry's stomach sank. There was no mistaking the betrayal in her tone. Now he understood the anger. Her husband had been going to the Caribbean with another woman. Henry's heart ached for Olivia. He could imagine how heartbroken she must be by not only her husband's death but his unfaithfulness. "I'm sorry. That must have been a shock. Do you want to talk about it?"

For a moment, she held herself stiff. Then she seemed to deflate as if all the air had been leached out of her lungs. He didn't like seeing her defeated.

She rested an elbow on the table and her chin in her hand. "I'm sure you don't want to hear my sad tale."

"You know everything there is to know about me. It would be kind of nice to know something about you."

She opened her mouth to speak, then hesitated. Her eyes widened and she straightened as if someone had poked her in the back. "No. No, no. We're not doing this."

He studied her now shuttered expression. "Doing what?"

"Getting personal." Her finger toggled between them. "You and me. I only know what the reports tell me, and what I've observed about you. We can't get personal, you know this."

He liked that the determined spark was back in her eyes, but he wanted her to be real with him because he had a feeling she didn't let her guard down often. He shouldn't pursue his curiosity—and whatever else was causing the warmth in his chest when he was around her. She was off-limits. Taboo. But what had always trying to do the right thing done for him? Couldn't he do what he wanted for once?

He set his empty plate aside and leaned forward. "Right at this moment, you're not IA and I'm not the officer you're investigating. Can't we just be two people, friends, who need to unload some baggage?"

The yearning on her face belied the negative shake of her head. She glanced around before meeting his gaze again. "No. There are too many eyes on us. On me. I can't mess this up. Not for you or anyone else."

She scooted her chair back from the table. Cody scrambled to his feet. "In fact, we should head back to the precinct so I can finish asking you questions about the previous excessive force case."

At least she was keeping her head, because he'd apparently lost his mind. Of course they couldn't get personal. Doing so put both their careers in jeopardy.

He stood up and turned the chair back around and shoved it up against the table. He had to refrain from holding out his hand so that she could hold on to him while she maneuvered out from behind the table.

For some reason, today her little baby bump seemed bigger. Or maybe she wasn't trying to hide it quite as much. He kept the observation to himself. She'd already made it clear her personal life was off-limits. Though he hated to think of the stress she must carry. A dead husband who was flying off with a woman Olivia hadn't known, and now a baby on the way to raise alone.

Not alone, he amended to himself as he and Cody followed her out of the pizzeria. She had her family. Family was everything.

On the sidewalk, he plucked his sunglasses from his pocket and slipped them on. They walked in silence with three feet separating them and Cody walking on his other side toward the K-9 unit headquarters. His phone chimed with an incoming text. His muscles tensed. Grabbing the device, he braced himself.

How many cops does it take to stop a bomber from blowing up your new girlfriend's house? None, because you can't! LOLZ

The words on the screen made his heart rate rev into overdrive. Who was the bomber targeting now?

Olivia stepped closer to Henry to read the words on the screen. Her mind raced. She hadn't seen any evidence that Henry had a girlfriend. If he did have one, Olivia needed to talk to her. And why did the thought of him dating cause a burning in her chest?

She frowned. "What's with this *LOLZ* thing? I get that this is texting lingo, but what does the *Z* stand for? I assume the *LOL* is *laugh out loud* and not *lots of love*."

Henry scoffed. "Yeah. I looked up text slang and apparently it means laughing out loud—hard. It has to be one of Davey's friends." He started them walking again at a fast clip. "And I don't know what he's talking about. A new girlfriend?" He shrugged his shoulders. "I haven't dated in years. Not since my last girlfriend gave me an ultimatum—her or Riley. I have no plans of getting into any relationship until Riley's out of the house and independent."

Conflicting emotions jumped inside Olivia. He wasn't dating anyone and he had no plans to. A true shame, because Henry would be an ideal catch. Responsible, protective, a man of faith. Any woman in her right mind would jump at the opportunity to snag him.

Not her, for course, even if she were in the market to try romance again. Which she wasn't, for so many reasons, including her chosen career. She was bringing a child into the world and her baby would need all of her focus. But wouldn't it be wonderful to have a partner to share her life with?

And his last girlfriend had given him an ultimatum? The nerve. Good riddance to that lady.

He stared at the phone as if he could find some meaning in the text. "I don't know what to make of this."

"Obviously, this suspect is mistaken. Could they be targeting the wrong person?"

Henry halted midstride. Cody turned sharply to look at his handler. With horror in his dark eyes, Henry stared her. "You. The suspect must mean you."

She scrunched up her nose. "What? Me? We're not dating!"

"I know, and you know, but the bomber doesn't. The guy saw us at the museum together and at the church together, and now here..." His gaze roamed the street. "He must be watching us. How else would he know that we're together right now?"

"You're making a big leap there. You don't know that he's talking about me." Yet she was totally creeped out by the thought of being stalked.

"You're the only woman I've spent any time with in forever."

The bomber thought they were together as a couple. Henry's logic made sense in a strange way. They had been together often the past few days. And each time something bad had happened. "Oh no. My neighbors. We have to get them out."

With his free hand, he grabbed hers. "Let's go."

Mind reeling, she ran alongside him and Cody. As soon as they reached the station, Henry ushered Olivia and Cody inside to raise the alarm. His boss was out on a call.

The station dispatcher promised to send the bomb squad and officers to Olivia's building.

Henry's dark eyes bored into her. "Olivia, you should stay here. Stay safe."

His concern burrowed deep inside of her. And as much as she appreciated his worry for her well-being, there was no way she was being left behind. "Not happening. I'm going with you. Let's hustle."

She heard his growl of frustration as she hurried for the exit.

Once secured inside the SUV, he called his boss and put it on speakerphone. Olivia's heart raced and she prayed for the people in her building. They didn't deserve to be in harm's way because she'd let herself become too involved with Henry and his sister.

"Sutherland," Gavin answered.

"Sir, we have a situation." Henry explained about the latest text, that he, Cody and Olivia were headed to her Carroll Gardens apartment building and that dispatch had already sent out an alert.

"I'm knee-deep here, but I trust you to handle this as supervisor of the scene. If that's acceptable to the lieutenant," Gavin said.

"Yes. I agree." Wholeheartedly. She

trusted Henry and Cody to sniff out any sort of explosive device.

"Be safe," Gavin said.

"Yes, sir." Henry hung up and started the engine.

Olivia couldn't believe what was happening. A strange sense of déjà vu gripped her as the K-9 unit vehicle tore out of the parking lot with the siren blaring.

When they arrived at her building, two patrol cruisers were already there and had set up a perimeter. One officer was talking with the superintendent. A fire truck rolled up with an ambulance, both at the ready. None could make a move until the location of the bomb was discovered and the threat assessed.

Henry put his hand on her arm before she could climb out of the vehicle. "No disrespect intended, but please stay put. Let Cody and I do our job. If our texting bomber has really put an explosive device in or around your apartment, we'll find it."

She had no doubt about their capability to detect a bomb. But she wasn't going to sit inside the car like some timid civilian. This was what she'd signed up for. Helping others. "I'm coming with you."

His jaw firmed. "Olivia, think about—"

"No." She jumped out and hurried up the walkway to the building's entrance.

Henry and Cody caught up to her. Cody's nose twitched and he skidded to a halt. The dog sat on the stoop and stared up at his partner.

"He's alerting."

There were no waiting packages or anything out of the ordinary. The planter with the bonsai tree that the superintendent maintained appeared undisturbed. As did the welcome mat. "Where's the explosive?"

He drew her and Cody away from the entrance to where the officers and other emergency personnel stood. To the superintendent, Henry asked, "Did you come out through the front entrance?"

"I did a couple of hours ago," the balding man replied. "I just returned from the hardware store when these officers rolled up."

"We didn't see anyone suspicious around the building," one of the officers said.

"The front door could be wired. Opening it might trigger the bomb."

Urgency made Olivia's heart rate double. "There are people inside. What if one of them decides to come out the front door? And Kitty! We have to get them out."

Henry nodded. "Is there a rear exit?"

"Yes, through the laundry room." The superintendent handed over his keys.

"Keep anyone from approaching the front entrance," Henry told the officers. To the emergency squad, he said, "Come with me."

"I'll show you the way," Olivia said, not about to let him sideline her. She led the way around the back of the building to a short staircase and the door leading into the laundry room. She and the others hung back while Henry let Cody sniff around the door and surrounding area. The dog didn't alert. Henry gave the all clear.

They raced inside with Cody in the lead. They moved through the building, banging on doors as they went, telling the few people home during the middle of the day to leave through the back exit.

Olivia opened the door to her apartment and rushed inside. "Kitty, Kitty!"

Cody entered, sniffing, made a beeline for her front window and sat staring at them.

"He's alerting," Henry declared. "The explosive is attached to your apartment window. We have to get out of here!"

"Not without my cat!" Panic fueled her. She ran to her bedroom where Kitty liked to hang out. The feline was curled on Olivia's pillow. Grabbing the cat, Olivia ignored its howling protest and ran with Henry and Cody. They relayed the bomb's location to the emergency personnel.

The officers had ushered the residents to a safe distance upwind of the building.

Henry conferred with the bomb squad technicians, one of whom was dressed in an explosive ordnance disposal suit. The other technician then brought out a bomb disposal robot and used a hand controller to send the robot across the sidewalk toward Olivia's front window.

Henry urged her forward to join her neighbors. They'd only made it a few steps when Henry's cell phone dinged, stopping them both in their tracks. Dread gripped Olivia as she pressed close to Henry to read the incoming text.

KaBOOM!

No sooner had the words registered than the window of Olivia's apartment exploded in a deafening bang, spitting glass a good ten feet.

Henry folded Olivia and Kitty into his arms away from the blast, while keeping Cody safely in front of him. Olivia burrowed into Henry's chest. Despite the fear, she felt safe in his arms. Unexpected, thrilling and terrifying all at once.

The last echo of the explosion left the world muffled. Henry leaned back to meet her gaze. "Are you okay?"

Her knees were wobbly. "I am. You?"

She remembered the last time they'd been in this position and though he'd reassured her about his state of being after the garbage can exploded, in actuality he had been injured. She inspected him carefully and saw no new wounds. Thankfully, the one on his scalp was healing.

Olivia turned to see that her front window had been blown out. The rest of the building looked unharmed. The bomb disposal robot appeared undamaged. After a careful inspection to make sure there were no additional explosive, the technicians and emergency personnel rushed forward.

Henry and Olivia moved out of the way to allow the others to work.

"I don't get it." Henry rubbed a hand over his jaw. "If this has something to do with Davey Carrell's injuries, why would the person come after you?"

"Remember what my attacker at the museum said? I'm supposed to find you guilty," Olivia reminded him. "This was just to show that he could get to me as easily as he could get to you. He seems bent on destruction rather than harm."

He shot her a look filled with disbelief.

"Remember the kids at Coney Island? They only suffered minor injuries and one broken bone, but still, it could have gone very differently if we hadn't arrived in time."

"True." Her stomach curdled. "But the bomber gave you time, just as he did here. He could have blown the window when we were on the building's stoop." And been cut up by flying glass.

"He may not intend to kill, but he certainly is intending harm," Henry said. "And given that you're pregnant..."

She sucked in a breath and held up a hand. "What makes you say that?" She'd known he suspected it but for him to state the fact was an entirely different matter. She'd tried too hard to conceal her growing abdomen.

"I heard your sister ask you about the baby." He shrugged. "I've noticed other things, as well."

Resigning herself to him knowing her secret, she said, "My family knows, but I haven't said anything to anyone else. My doctor cleared me for duty. I don't want anyone treating me differently because I'm expecting."

"I would imagine it's a bittersweet blessing," he said.

"It was definitely unexpected." Not wanting him to think she resented her baby, she added, "And a blessing. I know God has a plan. For me and this child. I just have to have enough faith to see it through."

"He always does have a plan," Henry said. "I love the verse Jeremiah 29:11, about God knowing the plans He has for us. I repeated it often after my father's death. Though sometimes the plan is uncomfortable and even painful."

They shared a common bond of loss. Somehow that seemed to tether her to him in unexplainable ways. She adjusted Kitty in her arms. "Roger and I were on the verge of a divorce and I had pretty much given up my hope of motherhood."

"I'm sorry to hear that," he said.

"I never imagined life would turn out so upside down. For so long, I tried to keep my marriage together, be the good wife. But nothing seemed to please Roger. He always found fault. I couldn't measure up to his ideal."

Henry frowned. "Why should you have had to measure up? That's not how love works."

Tears misted in her eyes. She blinked them back. Was Henry a man who would accept the woman he loved as she was, without expecting her to change to meet his wants and needs? Her heart throbbed with a longing that took her breath away.

"How far along are you?"

Pulling her composure around her like a cloak to ward off the flood of emotions clogging her throat, she forced out the words. "Nearly four months. I found out a month after Roger's death." She gave a wry twist of her lips. "I thought my morning sickness was stress and grief." And anger, but she didn't like what that said about her. "My mom convinced me to go to the doctor."

"That must have been a surprise."

"Yes." She nuzzled Kitty. "I have to admit the idea of raising a child by myself is daunting."

"You have your family for support and God to guide you," he said.

"True." She met his gaze. "But he or she will be my sole responsibility."

He reached forward to stroke Kitty's head. "I have complete faith you can do this, Olivia."

His words seeped into her, filling all the bruised places. She'd always wanted a family of her own, including a husband who would love her without conditions. If only Henry could be that man. But that couldn't happen. Even if she wasn't investigating him and they were free to pursue a relationship, he'd already made it clear he wasn't interested in being a parent again.

She really needed to find a way to put some distance between them. And not just physically, but emotionally, as well.

Henry's gaze moved to the building. "Did you live here with your late husband?"

It was a fair question. "After Roger's death, I couldn't stand to be in the home we'd shared. I had movers box up everything and sent Roger's items to his parents in Maine. I sold the apartment and rented this place."

Empathy softened the hard angles of Henry's handsome face. He touched her arm in a soothing gesture that made her want to lean on him for support. She refrained. Distance, remember?

"You can't remain here, obviously," Henry pointed out. "You'll come stay with Riley and me. Until this guy is caught."

The idea of living under the same roof as Henry sent her pulse jumping. That was one sure way for them both to get fired. Her investigation would be beyond compromised. "No way. It would be a conflict of interest for me to room with you and your sister. I'll be fine at a hotel for a few days."

The screech of tires on pavement drew Olivia's gaze. A police cruiser stopped and her father climbed out. Tall, with broad shoulders, Captain Alonso Vance scanned the crowd, his gaze locking on his daughter like a missile.

Grimacing, Olivia muttered, "Uh-oh. Brace yourself."

TEN

Olivia's father's long legs carried him to her side and he engulfed her in a hug. She inhaled the spicy scent of her father's aftershave and melted against him. Kitty meowed and squirmed to be set free.

After a moment, he stepped back. "Are you hurt?"

"No, Papa," she said, using her childhood nickname for him. At that moment, she wanted nothing more than to be his little girl and know he would make the world right.

"Thank you, God. I prayed the whole way over. I needed to make sure you were okay." Her father reached past her to offer Henry his hand. "Detective Roarke. Thank you for sending word."

Henry shook his hand. "Of course, Captain Vance."

"Wait, what?" She stared at Henry.

His matter-of-fact expression let her know he had no remorse for contacting her father. "While you were giving your statement, I had someone let your dad know what was happening."

Her emotions bounced between betrayal and being touched by the gesture. She didn't need anyone rescuing her. She wasn't some princess in a tower. She was an officer of the law. And Henry's superior. He shouldn't have taken it upon himself to alert her father.

"This is unacceptable, Olivia," her father said. "This suspect has to be caught."

Like she had any control of the situation? "We're working on it, Papa."

Her father's dark eyebrows rose. "Is that so? Since when does IA investigate bombings?"

"When the one targeted is the subject of an investigation. And now I've been targeted, as well." There was a heat in her tone that she'd rarely used with her father. But at the moment, she wasn't going to let her father or anyone else make her feel bad for doing her job. "This situation ties into the assault charge brought against Detective Roarke."

Her father's brown-eyed gaze vaulted from her to Henry. "I see."

Olivia frowned, not sure she liked the assessing look in her father's eyes. What exactly did he "see"?

"Detective Roarke, I will leave it to you to make sure the lieutenant is delivered safely to her family home. I'd do it myself but I have to return to the precinct."

"Yes, sir," Henry replied, surprised evident in his eyes.

Gaping at her father, Olivia couldn't believe what she'd just heard. "Excuse me. I'm right here. I'll stay in a hotel."

"Uh, no. Your mother would be livid," her dad stated. "You'll be safest at home." He reached to pet Kitty. "Both of you."

Though she hated to admit it, her father was right. Her parents' house was a fortress in many ways, with a state-of-the-art security system her father had installed a few years ago. Every inch of the property was covered with video cameras and motion detectors. Her father was beyond cautious. "Fine, but I can get myself home, thank you."

Her father leveled a stern look on her. "Not tonight. You aren't to be alone until this maniac is apprehended." Turning back to Henry, he continued, "You're welcome to stay for dinner. The whole family's coming. And Simone is making empanadas and *arroz con gandules.*"

Since when did Mama make her specialty dishes when it wasn't a holiday?

Henry grinned. "I can't leave my sister to fend for herself."

"The more the merrier," her father said. He turned back to her. "I'll let your mother know you're all right and will be coming to stay at the house." He walked away.

Olivia stared after him. What just happened? Why on earth would her father invite Henry over for dinner?

Her dad would be first in line of those

who'd want to lecture her on keeping her work separate from her personal life. Especially when it involved someone she was officially investigating.

Her brain was muddled with confusion. Maybe she had sustained a blow to the head after all during the explosion to her apartment window. Or she was just hormonal. Pregnancy could do that to a woman, right?

Because nothing was making sense at the moment. Certainly not the excitement and trepidation warring within her over Henry coming home for dinner. On the bright side, maybe having him under her parent's roof would help to clarify some of his behavior.

Or make things worse for her.

So much for keeping her distance from the too-handsome officer.

Apparently, Henry liked playing with fire. Why else would he have agreed so readily to join the Vance family for dinner?

He really should have begged off attending, but here he was. He glanced at Olivia in the passenger seat next to him. There was no reason for him and Riley to intrude on a family dinner. Olivia would be safe with her siblings and father. He and his sister's presence would only complicate matters. They would be the outsiders. Riley was already too emotionally involved with Olivia.

But the fact was, he liked Olivia and wanted to spend time with her and her family.

The thought tore through him like a bullet, blowing holes in all of his excuses.

Shaking his head at his own folly, he parked behind an older-model SUV in front of a two-story home in the Randall Manor neighborhood of Staten Island. "Nice place."

Riley, sitting in the back, leaned forward to stare out the side window. "This is where you grew up?"

"Yes, it is nice. A wonderful place to grow up," Olivia replied. She chewed her bottom lip as she too stared at her childhood home. Kitty lay curled in a borrowed cat carrier at Olivia's feet, oblivious to her human's anxiety.

Olivia hadn't said much since they'd met

with Gavin and filled him in on what had happened at her apartment before leaving the station.

Henry could tell his boss was stressed. Gavin's usually unflappable demeanor had cracked slightly as he'd made it clear he wanted Henry and Olivia to be extra careful. He'd even instructed Henry to stick close to Olivia and make sure nothing happened to her. This contradicted his earlier admonishment, but Henry hadn't pointed that out.

Instead, Henry had promised he would take every precaution to ensure both of their safety, which earned him a startled glance from the IA lieutenant. He'd expected her to protest, but she'd only nodded.

Now Henry laced his fingers through hers. "If you'd rather we didn't come in, I'd understand."

She turned to look at him, her pretty face softening and the worry dissolving. She tightened her grip around his hand. "I appreciate that. But Dad invited you and he'd be disappointed if you didn't show up."

"What about you?" Henry asked. "Do you want me—uh, us, here?"

Her lips parted and she inhaled sharply. Then she seemed to relax. Smiling, she said, "Yes. Of course. You and Riley and Cody are welcome."

Not exactly what he'd meant, but he'd take it.

They climbed from the vehicle and he hung back to let Cody wander on the front lawn on leash while Olivia tucked Riley's arm through hers and led her inside.

The neighborhood was quiet. Pleasant. Peaceful. Trees lined the sidewalks and family cars sat in driveways of dwellings similar to the Vance home. Henry had never lived in an actual house.

His parents had lived in a five-story walk-up in midtown until Henry's mother bailed. Then Henry's dad had married Susan and moved them to the condo in Brooklyn, where they lived when Riley came along. Something tightened in his chest.

A yearning for a suburban life like this caught him by surprise. What would it be like to have more space, like a garage with a workbench and storage?

The thought of her raising her baby alone made his heart ache. But there was nothing he could do for her. He wasn't prepared to take on the responsibility of parenting again, no matter how tempting it was to think of holding a baby and being there for all the early milestones.

He'd been too young and self-absorbed at sixteen to get excited about Riley's first words or steps or the first time she lost a tooth. Now she was his world.

"Cody, old boy, I think I need a vacation," Henry muttered.

"Do you?"

Henry whipped around to find Olivia a few feet away. She'd changed clothes. She now wore a loose dress that dropped below her knees to reveal nicely defined calves. Strappy sandals graced her feet. The sight of her pink painted toenails captivated him. She was such a contradiction from who he'd first assumed her to be. She could be uptight and rigid, strong and commanding, but she also had a sweetness to her that did funny things to his heart.

"Uh, yes. A vacation." Definitely needed to get away to clear his head. He shouldn't be so fascinated with Olivia. But there was so much to be fascinated by. Her regal bearing when she was working, her quick thinking, her protective instincts and her feisty spirit. She was wise and yet humble. All traits that he found appealing.

"I would agree," she said, taking a seat on the porch step. "Being targeted is maxing out my calm reserves."

Guilt poking at him, he sat down next to her. Cody settled at their feet. "I'm sorry you're in this mess."

"Not your fault. I'm doing my job. We all know there are those out there who would like to do any law enforcement officer harm. It's just a matter of time before someone bent on destruction takes notice of anyone on the job."

"Maybe, but you wouldn't be in this position if…"

If what? What could he have done or

changed that would have altered their circumstances? He'd had no control over Davey Carrell and his bogus accusations nor the serious health issues of the original IA officer, Lieutenant Jabboski, which had brought Olivia into the picture.

But Henry did have control over how much time outside of the station he'd spent with the lovely IA investigator.

His gut churned with remorse for putting her in harm's way needlessly. Especially because she was expecting a child.

But he couldn't find any regret for getting to know the beautiful lady.

"Hey." Olivia's soft voice drew him out of his thoughts. "We'll get through this. All of us."

But at what cost? His heart? His job? Her life? He couldn't let anything happen to Olivia.

Behind them, the front door opened and her brothers walked out. The two men stopped and stared.

"What are you two doing?" César Vance leaned against the porch post and grinned.

He was the younger of the two with a dark mustache, close-cropped dark hair and a trim build. He wore gym shorts and a T-shirt with the New York Knicks basketball logo. He looked like he was ready to head to the court.

Alexander Vance, on the other hand, looked ready for the golf course with gray shorts and a light-colored polo shirt. His frown made his rugged face rather fierce. He crossed his muscular arms over his broad chest. "Getting cozy with our sister, Roarke?"

"Knock it off, you two." Olivia rose to her feet and planted her hands on her hips. "We're just chatting."

"Chatting can lead to kissing," César sing-songed.

Henry scrambled to his feet, which prompted Cody to follow suit. "Don't be rude. I respect your sister too much to jeopardize her reputation or her career."

César lifted his hands. "Whoa. Dude, I was joking."

Embarrassed by his spontaneous reaction to his friend's words, Henry scrubbed a hand over his jaw. "Sorry. It's been a rough day."

"We heard," Alexander said. He unfolded his arms and drew his sister in for a brief hug. "We're glad you're both okay."

Olivia grinned at her eldest brother. "That's good to know."

"Mom says dinner in ten," Alexander said.

"We should go in and help." Olivia tugged on her brother's arm.

"You go on in," Alexander said. "We want to talk to Henry."

Olivia frowned. "I'm not sure that's a good idea."

"Worried about him?" César arched a dark brown eyebrow.

Henry's heart tumbled. What did she think was going to happen? That her brothers were going to beat him up? Not likely. "It's okay, Olivia. We'll be in shortly."

Olivia raised her index finger and pointed it at her each of her brothers. "Be nice."

With an apologetic look at Henry, she darted inside through the front door. Cody started after her but stopped at the length of his leash. Henry didn't blame the dog for wanting to escape with Olivia.

"So what gives?" César asked Henry as soon as the front door closed. "You and Olivia?"

Facing the two men, Henry hedged. "I'm not sure what you're talking about." Though he did, in fact, realize that his growing feelings for Olivia must be obvious to everyone. Except her. Or if she was aware, she was ignoring the attraction and affection filling the spaces between them. He would be wise to do the same.

Alexander stared him down. "We may be friends, but she's our little sister. Don't mess with her. She's had enough upheaval in her life lately and becoming involved with you could end her career."

Henry raised his hands. "I'm not messing with her. There's nothing happening between us. It's a professional relationship. She's investigating and I'm trying to help her. Trying to keep her safe."

"You may be telling yourself that," César

said, "but from where we're standing, things look like they're going in a direction that she doesn't need right now."

"I know she doesn't," Henry said. "The last thing I ever want to do is complicate Olivia's life."

But that seemed to be all he had done since he'd met her. The only way to remedy the situation was to bring the suspect who was targeting him to justice. Then Olivia would be free of the danger plaguing his every move. And she'd wrap up her investigation and they could part ways.

That last thought didn't settle well with him.

The front door opened and Captain Alonso Vance stepped out. He no longer wore his uniform. Now he was dressed in slacks and a short-sleeve button-down shirt. "All right, boys, that's enough. Henry is our guest. And dinner is ready."

"No worries, Pop," César said with a grin. "We're just giving Henry a hard time. All in good fun."

The glint in César's brown eyes belied his

words. Henry respected that Olivia's brothers wanted to protect her. He'd react exactly the same if it were Riley.

"That's right," Alexander said. "Henry's our friend and we know we can trust him."

He clapped Henry on the shoulder as they started to follow Alonso back in the house.

Before they entered, Alexander whispered, "Don't hurt her. Or you'll answer to us."

Henry acknowledged the words with a nod. "I don't plan to."

Once inside the house, Olivia tucked her arm through his and made the introductions. Gesturing to two women who couldn't have been more different, she said, "This is César's wife, Kerry Jo, and Alexander's wife, Rosie."

Kerry Jo was petite with wild, curly red hair and vivid green eyes. "It's nice to meet you." A heavy Texas twang clung to her voice. "Your sister is lovely."

"Thank you," Henry said. He spied Riley in the dining room helping Ally Vance set the large oval table. Having only ever seen

Ally in her paramedic uniform, it was a bit of surprise that dressing in casual clothes made her look nearly as young as Riley.

"Olivia says you two work together," Rosie said. Tall and athletic, the woman's dark hair hung below her waist and she held a sleepy toddler on her hip.

"Technically, Olivia is investigating Henry." The woman who entered the living room held out her hand to Henry. "Maria Vance. Olivia's other sister."

Henry grasped her hand and was surprised by the firm grip. "Nice to meet you."

"Hmm." Maria withdrew her hand, her golden brown eyes assessing him. She wore a tailored navy dress suit, a bright red collared blouse and red pumps, appearing every inch the assistant district attorney that she was. Henry had never had an occasion to work with her at the courthouse.

"And this is our mother." Olivia indicated the elder woman wiping her hands on a towel as she entered the room. Tall, striking and lithe, Mrs. Vance moved forward gracefully to shake his hand. The resemblance between Mrs. Vance and her daughters was unmistakable.

"Mrs. Vance, thank you for including Riley and me this evening," Henry said.

"Please, call me Simone," she said. "You're very welcome. I'm glad Alonso invited you. Can I get your dog a bowl of water?"

"That would be wonderful. Thank you, Simone." Henry led Cody to the water bowl she put down on the floor for him.

Ally waved to him from the dining room. Rosie and Alexander slipped down the hall and returned a few moments later without their child.

"Take your seats, everyone," Alonso said from the archway between the living room and dining area.

After settling Cody down near the door, Henry took a seat next to Riley. Olivia sat down on Henry's other side, which caused several speculative glances. Henry wasn't sure what to make of the Vance clan, but he had to admit it was nice to be included in the gathering.

When everyone was settled in their seats,

Alonso said a blessing over the food. "Lord, we thank You for this bounty and for the family and friends gathered close. We ask for Your protection, Your blessing and guidance. May we each be a blessing to You, Lord. Amen." Alonso smiled. "Dig in."

"This smells delicious," Henry said as he took an empanada from the platter Olivia passed to him.

"These are some of our favorite dishes from my home country," Simone said.

"My mother and her parents moved stateside from Puerto Rico when Mama was a little girl." Olivia explained.

"Mrs. Vance promised to teach me how to make empanadas," Riley told him with a wide smile.

Henry's heart swelled. He was grateful to the Vance family for being so welcoming to his sister.

Over the course of the next hour, he laughed, ate and swapped stories with the Vances. It was fun to see Olivia interacting in such a casual way with her family. The care and respect they showed each other was a testimony to the power of such a close-knit clan.

Sitting here with Olivia's family created a craving in Henry he'd never experienced. He liked this big, noisy family setting. He glanced at Olivia and met her gaze. The tender affection in her eyes flipped his heart over. It took all he had not to lean over and kiss her right there in front of her whole family. He was in way too deep.

After dinner, Henry offered to do the dishes. "It's the least I can to do after such a scrumptious meal."

"What a good idea, Henry," Alonzo Vance said with approval. "Gentlemen, the ladies cooked so we can clean."

"Oh man," César complained, though he gathered plates as he spoke. "Why did you have to go and offer?"

César's wife wrapped her arms around his waist. "Don't worry, honey. You won't lose your man card for doing some dishes."

Everyone laughed. Henry enjoyed doing the dishes with the Vance men. Despite the earlier tension, they had good conversations about the Mets, the Knicks and the state of the police force.

Once the kitchen was back in order, the family gathered in the living room, where Riley was looking at photo albums.

"Henry, you have to see these," Riley held up a picture of the Vance siblings as children, all dressed in matching outfits. Over the next hour, Henry was shown a history of the Vance family in photographs. He learned that even as a child, Olivia stood out among her siblings with the regal way she held herself. Finally the evening wore down. The siblings left and the elder Vances retired for the night, leaving Olivia, Riley and Henry in the living room.

A cell phone chimed. Henry's gut clenched. With dread eating a hole through his nerves, he reached in his pocket for his phone, fully expecting to see another taunting text from their mysterious bomber.

But it wasn't his phone that had chimed. It had been Riley's. She dug her phone out and stared at it for a moment with a scowl before sticking the device back in her backpack.

"Who was that?" Henry wanted to know who could make his little sister frown so fiercely.

She sighed. "Nobody."

"Well, I'm sure nobody has a name." Henry moved from where he'd been sitting in a straight back chair to plunk himself down next to Riley on the sofa. "What gives?"

"It's just somebody from school," Riley said. "It's no big deal."

"Is someone bothering you?" he pressed.

"No." Riley grabbed her backpack and stood. "Isn't it time for us to go home?"

Henry exchanged a concerned glance with Olivia. There was definitely something upsetting his sister. Was this the same person who had been texting her multiple times throughout the last few days?

But judging from the stubborn expression on his sister's face, he decided now wasn't the time to press her further.

Olivia took his hand. "I'll walk you out." His sister's raised eyebrows brought heat creeping up his neck, but he wasn't going to let go of Olivia until he had to.

At the front door, Olivia released her hold on him so he could leash Cody. "I'll talk to you tomorrow," he told her.

She gave a sigh that sounded resigned. "Yes. Tomorrow. Back to reality."

Riley took Cody's leash and opened the front door. "We'll step out if you want to kiss."

Henry's chest tightened. He wanted nothing more than to do as his sister suggested. But there were risks that needed to be considered. Lines that shouldn't be crossed. The stakes of giving into emotion were too high.

Olivia tilted her head up, her lips parted. An invitation?

Despite the multitude of reasons why he should step back, his head dipped, bringing his lips close to hers. He inhaled the floral scent clinging to her skin.

A sudden gasp had him jerking back.

"Henry!"

Riley's panicked voice galvanized him

into action. He raced out the door and skidded to a halt. Someone had vandalized the K-9 unit SUV.

ELEVEN

Olivia sucked in a sharp breath as horror
flooded her. In the glow of the porch light
there was no mistaking the red paint slashed
across Henry's K-9 unit vehicle. The word
pig was spelled out in big letters on the side
and the tires had been slashed. The SUV
listed to the side.

Henry's gaze roamed the darkened street.
"Cody and I will take a walk around the perimeter to make sure no one is lurking about
or left any explosives." He met Olivia's gaze.
"Keep my sister safe."

"I will." Her heart bumped against her
ribs. "This had to have happened recently
or my siblings would have said something
as they were leaving."

"Agreed."

She tugged Riley back into the house. "Be careful."

Henry flashed her a brief smile and a nod as he shut the door behind him, sealing them safely within the cocoon of her family home. That someone would deface the K-9 vehicle right outside the front door made Olivia shiver. Was this the bomber's latest ploy? Or something entirely different?

Riley stood frozen, her dark-eyed gaze unfocused on the closed door.

Compassion urged Olivia to wrap an arm around the younger woman's waist and draw her into the living room. "Come sit back on the couch."

A few moments later Henry and Cody returned. "All clear. You better get your dad," Henry said. The grim set of his jaw spoke of his upset at the malicious vandalism. "I'll call the local precinct."

Cody settled at Riley's feet as if the K-9 sensed she needed comforting. Olivia definitely wanted to get a dog.

Leaving Riley in Cody's care, Olivia hurried to her parents' room and lightly knocked on the door. "Dad, we have a problem."

After Olivia explained what had happened, her father and mother quickly joined her, Henry and Riley in the living room.

"Cody didn't alert, so there's that," Henry said. "At least this isn't an explosive situation."

"I'll check the recordings from the security cameras I have set up," her dad said and headed to his office down the hall. Henry followed in her dad's wake.

"I'll make some coffee," her mom said. "Riley, would you help me? I think we have some hot cocoa in the cupboard, as well."

Grateful to her mother for distracting Riley, Olivia hugged her mom then joined Henry and her dad in his den. Her father sat behind his desk, his fingers flying over the keyboard of his computer. The front porch came into view on the monitor. He rewound the footage to reveal a guy in a black hoodie and a neoprene face mask spray painting Henry's vehicle. There was no way to identify the culprit. He took off on foot down the street.

"Can you send this to Eden Chang at the Brooklyn K-9 Unit? Hopefully she can compare this guy to our bomber and see if they match in height and weight," Henry said. "Then we'll at least know if we're dealing with the same person."

"Did the museum ever send over their security camera feed?" Olivia asked. "This guy looks around the same build as the one who grabbed me."

"I'll ask Eden." Henry moved away to call the unit's technology expert.

Olivia put her hand on her dad's shoulder. "I'm sorry for bringing this home."

Her father swung his chair around to face her. "Nonsense. You are not at fault. Neither is Henry."

Her stomach quaked. "My investigation into Henry's case has been compromised."

Giving her an intense stare, he asked, "Can you be objective?"

"I don't know, Papa," she admitted. She had grown to care a great deal for Henry and Riley. Could even see herself falling for him if the circumstances were different.

"You must be." The decisive tone brooked no argument. He took her hands in his. "Let the facts speak. Take your emotions out of it. You have a good head on your shoulders. And you have really good instincts."

She blinked back sudden tears at his confidence in her abilities. "Thank you." She squared her shoulders. "I will do my job."

"That's all that is required of you."

Concern for the Roarke siblings' safety stuttered through her. "However, I do think Henry and Riley shouldn't go home tonight. There's plenty of room here."

Her father narrowed his gaze and seemed to toss the idea around in his head before saying, "Agreed. I'll leave it up to you to convince him."

Twisting her lips, she contemplated what she could say to persuade Henry that he and his sister would be safer here.

She cast a prayer heavenward that God would lend her a hand.

A commotion in the living room drew their attention.

"Sounds like the cavalry has arrived." Her father stood and tucked her arm through his and escorted her to greet the local law enforcement officers filling the entryway.

After giving their statements, Olivia joined her mother and Riley in the kitchen.

"Riley was telling me about the upcoming concert she's going to," her mom said. "I remember when you went to your first concert. Let's see, the band was…"

Olivia laughed. "Maroon 5. I had a crush on Adam Levine."

"Your sisters were so jealous that you got to go without them." Her mom's eyes twinkled.

"I remember. Maria and Ally wanted every detail about the concert. And wouldn't let me get any sleep that night."

"You were allowed to go alone?" Riley asked, her eyes hopeful.

"No," Olivia said. "My two brothers and their friends took me and a few of my friends."

"Oh." Riley's mouth turned into a pout.

Henry walked into the room just as Riley's phone chimed again. She dug it out of her backpack and glanced at the screen. Her lip curled and she deleted the message.

"Everything okay?" Henry asked her.

"Yes." She tucked the phone in her backpack.

Olivia shared a concerned look with Henry. That was the second text tonight to seemingly upset the young woman.

"Is someone bothering you?" Olivia asked.

A fleeting glimpse of panic crossed Riley's face before she pressed her lips together. "Seriously, it's no big deal. I can handle it."

Henry tugged his sister back on to the couch. "Riley, what's going on?"

"I'm allowed to have a life that doesn't involve you, Henry." Her tone had taken on a sullen note.

"Yes, you are," he said. "But whatever this text was, it upset you."

In fact, she looked a little scared. Acid churned in Olivia's midsection. "Riley, have any of your friends been acting strange lately? Have any of them been threatening you?"

Riley's gaze jumped to her. "No, it's nothing like that. This has nothing to do what's going on with Henry."

Olivia covered Riley's hand with her own. "You may not think it's connected, Riley, but it could be. The bomber followed you on the boardwalk."

"What? Why?" Fear clouded her eyes. "How does the bomber know who I am?"

"That's what we're trying to find out," said Henry. "I really need you to be straight with me and tell me if you can think of anyone who'd want to hurt you."

She jumped up and pushed past Henry, hurried to the bathroom and shut the door.

Henry moved to follow her, but Olivia held him back. "Let her have a moment."

"I worry about her," he said.

"Of course you do." One of the many reasons she was falling for him. His big heart. His generosity. His kindness. *Stop it!* She had to tame her emotions. "Why don't you let her stay the night here tonight? In fact, you both can stay. There's plenty of room. And I'd feel so much better having you and Cody here."

He hesitated a moment, surprise lighting the dark depths of his eyes. "You know, that would be helpful. I think she'd feel safer here with more people around than she would at home."

Grateful that God had granted her prayer, Olivia said, "Great. I'll talk to Riley when she's calmer. I've been meaning to, but with everything that's been going on…"

"Understandable. Don't feel bad. It's been a stressful few days."

Olivia gave him a quick nod, appreciating his thoughtfulness in letting her off the hook for not following through on her word. "I've also been meaning to address that old case with you. The domestic call six years ago."

"Right. What do you want to know?"

"I read the report and noted the date was close to the time you lost your father." She wanted to be sensitive to his loss, but she needed to understand.

Henry sat back down. "It was a week or so after."

"I would imagine you and Riley were struggling to adjust to your new normal."

"Yes. Our new normal." He seemed to ponder her words. "That first year was difficult."

"Why were you back in the field so soon?"

He frowned. "The department psychologist cleared me for duty."

"I saw that, but I wouldn't have thought you'd be ready."

He shrugged. "Not working wasn't going to help anyone. Riley and I had to keep functioning."

Her heart ached at the grief lacing his words. She understood the need to move on. Resuming her duties had kept her sane after Roger's death. "Can you tell me about that night? What happened?"

He ran a hand over his jaw. "A domestic call came in. I was on patrol with my partner at the time, Officer Maury Standeven.

Maury had been on the job for twenty years, he taught me a great deal about being an officer."

He paused as if remembering. "We were the first responders. The wife had been badly beaten. I was surprised she survived. The suspect, her husband, was enraged. We managed to pull him off his wife when a young kid stepped out of a closet. The husband went berserk. Knocked Maury over in his effort to get free. I got between him and the child. The suspect took a swing at me. Missed. My only option was to subdue him, which I did."

"And he claimed you used excessive force," she said. The story sounded too familiar. Could a six-year-old domestic case and the current one she was investigating be connected?

The bathroom door opened suddenly and Riley stepped out.

Henry stood. "You okay?"

"I'm fine," the young woman said.

Riley's chin jutted out in a stubborn way that Olivia was beginning to recognize.

Henry certainly had his hands full with his little sister, even if she was a grown woman now. Olivia could imagine the handful Riley had been as a young teen.

"We know you are," Olivia said. "You and Henry are going to stay the night."

"We are?" Riley appeared excited and relieved by the prospect.

"Come on, you two. I'll get you set up in the guest rooms." Olivia led the way to the two back bedrooms that had once been her brothers'. When they both married, Olivia's mom had converted their rooms into guest quarters. Alexander's old room had a crib in it for his son, Tyler. Cody sniffed every corner, then sat wagging, as if giving his approval.

"Henry, I'm sure dad has some clothes you can borrow for the night," she said. "I'll go ask him."

She returned a few minutes later with sweatpants and a T-shirt. "And the bathroom across the hall has extra toothbrushes in the cabinet below the sink. As well as fresh towels if you want to shower."

"We appreciate your hospitality," he said. He hugged Riley. "Try to rest. Take Cody with you. For extra security."

She hugged him back. "You rest, too."

Over her head, Henry smiled at Olivia. "Thank you."

She nodded as tenderness flooded her veins. She wanted a hug, too, but that would be too much to ask for and very inappropriate. Instead, she stepped out of the room and waited for Riley. Olivia showed her to the room next door. Cody did his sniffing routine then settled down at the foot of the bed.

Pulling a large T-shirt from the dresser, Olivia handed it to Riley. "You can sleep in this."

Taking the shirt, Riley sat on the bed. "This really stinks."

"The T-shirt?"

Riley laughed. "No." She lifted it to her nose. "Maybe a little."

"I'll get you one of mine." Horrified, Olivia held out her hand for the shirt.

"I can deal with it," Riley said and hugged the shirt to her chest. "I mean what's happening. Why would someone do that to the SUV?"

"We won't know what's motivating this person until we catch him."

"I worry about Henry," Riley said, her eyes big with anxiety. "What if someone hurts him? I can't lose him, too."

Olivia sat next to Riley and put an arm around her, wanting to assure the young woman that nothing would happen to her brother, but knowing she couldn't make such a promise. "Keep him in your prayers. Put your faith in God to protect him." She gave her a squeeze. "Henry's concerned about you, too."

"I know." Riley leaned into Olivia. "He's been really good to me. It's just he can be so controlling. And annoying."

"That's the thing about siblings," Olivia told her.

Riley pulled back to meet her gaze. "You and your brothers and sisters all seem to get along well."

Olivia made a face. "We haven't always. My brothers were protective and overbearing at times. While my sisters were wild and annoying. I love them all, though, and would do anything for all of them."

"But you went to concerts when you were eighteen. I'm an adult now. I shouldn't need Henry's permission."

Ah. The crux of the matter. "I did go and my brothers went with me. But I also lived here, in my parents' home. Even though I could legally vote and was expected to be responsible for my actions, I had to follow my parents' rules until I moved out."

Riley groaned.

"Your brother isn't trying to keep you from doing what you want to do, he only wants to make sure you're safe. With everything that's been going on, can you blame him?"

Riley made a face. "No. I get it. It's just frustrating."

Olivia understood the sentiment. "I don't like being coddled either. But sometimes we have to let those who love us protect us."

"I suppose you're right."

Taking the concession as a win, Olivia

asked, "Is that what the text was about? The concert?"

"Kind of," Riley said. "It was Parker Wilton. The guy you met at the museum. He wanted to know if I was going to the concert. He keeps asking me out and I keep telling him no."

Olivia's senses went on alert. "Has Parker been bothering you?"

Riley shrugged. "I don't want to date him. He is not my type."

Okay. Olivia wasn't going to touch the "type" comment. At the moment that was irrelevant. "So he's not taking no for an answer." She didn't like the sound of that.

"No, he's not. I finally told him that I wasn't going to date until I moved out because my brother's a cop and gives my dates too hard a time."

Olivia chuckled. She was sure Henry would approve. "And what was Parker's response?"

She wrinkled her nose. "He begged me to give him a chance. Am I being childish by not at least going to lunch with him?"

"What kind of guy is he?"

"He's nice enough. At least he was in the beginning. But after I turned him down a couple of times, he kind of became pushier. He rarely ever smiles now."

Concern arced through Olivia. "Have you told your brother?"

"Are you kidding me?" Riley shuddered. "Henry's in enough trouble. He doesn't need to deal with my stuff, too." Her expression was earnest as she said, "I'm not kidding when I say Henry would give my dates a hard time. When I was in high school, I went to the prom with Gerald Hamilton. When Gerald came to pick me up, Henry was cleaning his service weapon on the coffee table. Kind of freaked Gerald out."

Olivia pressed her lips together to suppress a smile as she pictured the scenario. That sounded like something her dad or brothers would have done. "I would imagine that was very intimidating for a high schooler."

"Yeah, you could say that. Gerald wouldn't talk to me the rest of the school year."

"That was Gerald's loss." Olivia tucked one of Riley's curls behind her ear. "You know, your brother is doing the best he can."

"Yes. I just wish he'd lighten up a little. He's always had to be totally in charge and on top of things. I'm afraid to make any mistakes because he expects perfection."

Olivia's heart squeezed tight. She could relate to the sentiment. Her parents had always expected great things, if not perfection, from their children. Especially her, as the oldest daughter. "I'm sure your brother knows you are less than perfect. We all are. But Henry once told me that love wasn't about measuring up to somebody else's expectations. I think he is a rare man who loves unconditionally."

Riley tilted her head and stared at Olivia. "You're right. He would be a great catch."

The comment elicited a startled laugh from Olivia. She needed to nip any ideas of matchmaking in the bud right now. "Yes, well. I'm sure one day he will find the right person. Now, I'm going to let you go to sleep. If you need anything, your brother is right next door. And I'm on the second floor right above you."

"Thank you. Hey, I just had an idea," Riley said. "What if you come with Henry when he escorts me and my friends to the concert? Then you two could go on a date."

Oh, dear. Riley wasn't going to give up easily. "I can't date your brother. It's against the rules. But maybe I could go with you."

"I'd like that."

Olivia wasn't so sure Henry would. "Good night." She shut the door quietly.

"Is everything okay?"

Startled, Olivia put her hand over her heart. There was just enough ambient light for her to see Henry leaning against the wall. He was wearing a pair of Alex's lounge pants and a T-shirt. His feet were bare. The scent of mint and soap wound around her. Attraction pulled at her like a riptide in the ocean.

To prevent herself from stepping into his arms, she leaned back against the wall opposite him. "Yes, everything will be fine. The person texting your sister is Parker Wilton. The guy we saw talking to her at the museum."

Henry pushed away from the wall. "He's harassing her?"

"More like trying to convince her to go out on a date with him."

Henry harrumphed. "We'll see about that."

His protectiveness was endearing. "Tomorrow I would suggest doing a background check on him, just to be safe. And maybe you should sit down and talk to Riley. She seems to be under the impression she has to be perfect for you."

He exhaled as if her words were a punch to the gut and straightened away from the wall. "Maybe I should talk to her right now."

Olivia stepped into his path. She placed her hand over his heart. She could feel the heat from his skin coming through the T-shirt. The thump of his heart beat against her palm. Her mouth dried. She licked her lips, then said, "It's late. We all need our rest."

He placed his hand over hers, curling his fingers around it to hold it in place. "You're right. Again. You have an amazing way of grounding me."

"Is that a good thing?" Why did her voice sound so breathless?

Her pulse beat at a staccato tempo. Standing here with him, shrouded in the hallway shadows, she could almost pretend the rest of the world didn't exist. She couldn't remember ever being so drawn to a man before in such an elemental way.

She'd found her late husband attractive and had loved him, once. But he'd never made her heart pound with such giddy anticipation. She pushed the thoughts of her past away. They had no place in the here and now.

"It's a very good thing," Henry murmured. "And a dangerous one."

She understood exactly what he meant. But the thread of attraction knitting them together was stronger than her will. In this moment, she was helpless to resist the yearning deep in her soul.

Going on tiptoe, she pressed her lips to his.

The kiss was sweet and gentle but electrifying in a way that brought tears to her eyes.

Then his free hand tangled in her hair, cradling the back of her head as he deepened the kiss. Some part of her realized her world was on the verge of change even as internal alarms bells clanged a loud warning.

Slowly, he eased back until their lips separated. He dropped his forehead to hers. "I better say good-night now."

She wanted to protest. She wanted nothing more than to just stay here in this space, this moment, for as long as possible.

Something nudged her ankle and a soft meow shattered the intimate circle surrounding her and Henry.

Stepping back, she picked up Kitty and cradled the feline in her arms. The cat was a poor substitute for the attractive man standing before her.

"Good night, Henry." Olivia hurried to the safety of her room upstairs.

Her cat may be a poor substitute, but at least Kitty wouldn't cost Olivia her career.

TWELVE

The next morning, Henry was awake long before the sunrise. He'd had a fitful night thinking about a certain IA lieutenant.

Because his SUV had been towed to the crime scene lab, Olivia and her father drove him and Riley to their condo. Henry changed into his uniform while Cody ate his kibble and Riley got ready for her summer class. Henry was grateful that Riley didn't protest when a plainclothes officer arrived to escort her to school.

Captain Vance then dropped Olivia, Henry and Cody off at the K-9 unit headquarters with a warning to be careful.

They stood side by side outside the entrance for a long moment after her father's car drove away. Henry understood they needed to discuss the kiss, but he was afraid if they talked about it, any discussion would somehow lessen the moment and force them to come to terms with breaking the rules.

All night, he'd wrestled with his conscience over allowing the intimacy. He'd put her career at risk. Not to mention his own. Yet he didn't regret kissing her, not when doing so had felt so right, so natural. The kiss was imprinted on his memory. Something he'd never forget. But also that he'd never repeat.

"I hope you—" he said.

"I was thinking—" Olivia said at the same time.

Henry chuckled. "Please, ladies first."

"Okay. I think we need to run a background check on Parker Wilton."

Henry studied her for a moment. That wasn't at all what he'd expected her to say, but he'd go with it. Back to work. Better to keep the professional wall up. "Okay. It might be best if we have Eden run it."

"Good," Olivia said. "I need to speak with

her anyway. You can make the introduction."

He led her to Eden's office. The technology expert was at her desk and she swiveled her chair around as they entered.

"Well, hello," Eden said.

"Eden, this is Lieutenant Olivia Vance," Henry said.

Eden's eyes widened and she stood. "Nice to meet you." Her curious gaze turned to Henry. "What can I do for you?"

"We were hoping you could pull some information about a young man named Parker Wilton," Olivia responded, drawing Eden's focus. "He's a person of interest in a case."

Henry's eyebrows shot up. Did she think this kid had something to do with the vandalism last night? Or the bombing? Riley had met Parker in her summer college class, after the incident with Davey Carrell.

Eden resumed her seat and her fingers flew over her keyboard. "Let's see," Eden said. "Parker Wilton. Age nineteen. No criminal record. Mom, Karen Wilton. Also no criminal record." She hit a button and her printer whirred, then spit out a sheet of paper. "Here's the home address."

"Thank you," Olivia said, taking the page and handing it to Henry. "I have some other questions for Eden. We need a moment alone."

"Uh, sure. We'll wait in the hall." Henry stared at the paper as he and Cody exited Eden's office. Parker lived in Red Hook. Something pinged at the back of his brain.

He grew antsy as he waited for Olivia to finish speaking with Eden. He hoped the unit's technology expert told Olivia her theory that he was being set up. Plus, he needed to have Eden do another search.

Finally, the office door opened. He pounced before Olivia could walk out.

"Eden, could you look up Davey Carrell's home address?"

"Detective Roarke." The censure in Olivia's tone echoed on the small space. "You are not going there. You know you have to stay away from anything to do with Carrell."

"Bear with me, here. I have a suspicion and I need to see if I'm right," he said.

Eden shrugged and sat down at her computer again. "Hmm. Seems Davey Carrell's family also lives in Red Hook."

"What high school did Davey and Parker attend?" Henry asked.

"Just because they live in the same section of the city doesn't mean the two young men know each other," Olivia pointed out.

Eden's fingers flew over the keyboard. "They both graduated from South Brooklyn Community High School."

Henry turned to Olivia. "We need to talk to Parker and Davey."

She stared at him for a long moment. "You're right. But you can't go near Davey. I was planning to interview him anyway. I'll go to both of their homes and talk to them."

"I can talk to Parker," Henry said.

"I don't think that's a good idea," Olivia countered.

"Hey." Detective Bradley McGregor popped his head inside the doorway. "Henry,

I heard what happened to your K-9 vehicle. That's just unbelievable."

"Yeah, I doubt Gavin's going to be too happy with me," Henry said.

Olivia frowned at him. "He can hardly blame you for the vandalism."

Henry shrugged. "Still, it happened on my watch, in my possession."

Olivia arched an eyebrow. "There are just some situations in life you cannot control."

"Spoken like somebody who knows," he quipped, remembering Olivia's comment about her own need for control.

Bradley chuckled, his gaze bouncing between them with a speculative gleam. "You two are funny. Gavin's called an emergency staff meeting. He wants us all there."

Eden rose from her chair. "We're coming." She shooed Henry and Olivia out of her office. "Move it, you two. You can debate who's going where after the meeting."

Henry and Olivia followed Bradley and Eden, but when Olivia stopped in the hallway, Henry walked back to her side as the other two disappeared into the conference room.

Henry searched Olivia's pretty eyes. "Are you coming?"

She worried her bottom lip. He was captivated by the way her teeth tugged on the tender flesh and he wanted to kiss away her worry. That was so not going to happen.

"I kind of intruded on the last one."

"You didn't intrude. You made a sound suggestion." Henry held out his hand for her to take. "You're more than welcome. Come on."

She eyed his hand then gave him a very stern look. "Henry, we need to keep things professional."

Though her words stung, he appreciated that she was drawing a boundary. He saluted her. "Yes, Lieutenant."

She made a face at him. "Smart aleck."

He chuckled and held the door open for her. Henry and Cody walked in behind Olivia and edged to the left of the doorway, finding a spot to stand against the wall. Olivia hesitated, then moved to stand beside him. She gave him a sheepish glance that had him wanting to put an arm around her and hug her close.

Instead, he crossed his arms over his chest and paid attention to his boss, Gavin, who stood at the podium at the front of the room. He had dark circles under his eyes. Apparently he'd pulled an all-nighter.

"Listen up, everyone," Gavin said, drawing the attention of the group gathered. "Despite a patrol car parked outside Officer Noelle Orton's house every night for the past few months, last night someone attempted to break in to steal Liberty. Noelle called for backup and we had the house surrounded within minutes. This was a win. We caught the guy."

Henry would have liked to have been in on that takedown. Liberty was one of their best K-9s, a yellow lab whose detection work, particularly in stopping gun smugglers, had prompted the bounty. Unfortunately, the light-colored dog had one black splotch on an ear that made her an easy target. Henry couldn't stand the thought of someone hurting one of their dogs or their officers. But he had had his own incident to deal with last night.

Gavin continued, "When we interrogated the suspect, we confirmed that there is a ten-thousand-dollar bounty on Liberty's head. Of course, we've known this from informants and because there have been several attempts on Liberty's life, but this is the first time we've gotten it straight from a suspect's mouth. We cut a deal with the suspect and promised to process him out of state if his intel leads to the arrest of the person who put out the hit on Liberty. The suspect says he only knows the gunrunner by the name of Gunther and that he operates out of Coney Island."

Gavin's gaze locked on to Henry. "Henry's vehicle was also vandalized last night. Our unit is under attack. We must be vigilant at all times, people. On another note," Gavin said, "Thanks to the suggestion of Lieutenant Olivia Vance, the FBI has put Agent Caleb Black on the McGregor and Emery murders."

Beside Henry, Olivia made a pleased little noise in her throat. He bumped his shoulder into her and whispered, "Told you. Good idea."

Though she didn't acknowledge him, she smiled and kept her gaze on Gavin.

"Agent Black caught a break quickly and reported that he'd intercepted Randall Gage, whose DNA puts him at the crime scene of the McGregors' murder—"

Several members of the K-9 unit cheered.

Gavin held up his hand and waited until it was quiet. "Unfortunately, Gage managed to evade Agent Black and escaped. This happened upstate in the Catskills."

A grumble swept through the room.

"Agent Black has vowed to continue to track Gage and keep us apprised of his progress," Gavin finished. "Now, I want all of you to be extra careful out there. Dismissed."

Henry pushed away from the wall as Gavin called out, "Henry, Lieutenant Vance, hold up."

A chill of apprehension slithered down his

spine. Had his boss somehow found out that he and Olivia... No, of course not. Still, tension knotted his shoulders. "Yes, sir."

Gavin waved over Officer Lani Jameson and her dog, Snapper. While Gavin conferred with Lani, Henry led Cody out of the path of officers exiting the room.

Olivia sidled up to him and asked in a hushed tone, "What do you think he wants?"

"Probably to know when you're going to file your report." He cringed at the sharpness of his tone.

Her eyebrows dipped and her expression hardened. "Soon."

"Good to know." He didn't understand his sudden irritation. Or maybe he did. Guilt. Guilt for kissing her. Guilt for having feelings for the IA investigator that could land them both in hot water. He ran a hand over his shaved head in an ineffective effort to relieve the pressure building there, warning that a migraine was brewing.

Officer Noelle Orton and her K-9 partner, Liberty, stopped beside Henry. Cody scrambled to his feet but stayed in place.

The other dog, a beautiful yellow lab with a big, black smudge on her left ear, ignored Cody and sat at Noelle's side.

"Lieutenant, have you met Officer Orton?" Henry asked.

"We have not had the pleasure." Olivia shook hands with Noelle.

"Noelle is a rookie with our unit. She is a former trainer at the NYC K-9 Command Unit in Queens. Several months ago, she and her partner, Liberty, foiled two military-weapon gun smuggling operations worth millions at Atlantic Terminal. Ever since, that bounty Gavin mentioned in the meeting, has been on Liberty's head."

"Well done," Olivia told Noelle.

Noelle gave her a slight smile and nodded. Henry had the distinct feeling Noelle wasn't too happy. Though having a bounty on your partner would do that.

As soon as the room was clear, Gavin moved from the podium to stand in front of Henry. Lani and Snapper hung back as if waiting for further instructions.

To Henry, Gavin said, "You're to stick

close to the station for the foreseeable future. Hannah is expecting you in the training center. You'll work with Noelle and Liberty among others today."

Henry glanced at Olivia. "But what about Oliv—I mean Lieutenant Vance?" His boss had told him to keep her safe. Henry didn't like the idea of her working alone.

"We've got that covered," Gavin said. He focused on Olivia. "Lieutenant, I've spoken to your superior officer. And he is in agreement. Lani and Snapper will provide you backup while you are conducting your investigation."

Henry rolled this new development around in his mind. He trusted Lani and had no doubt that Snapper would be protective of both his handler and Olivia. That was what the dog was trained for, after all.

Gavin continued, "Your father would like extra precautions taken to guarantee your well-being."

Olivia gaped at the sergeant. Henry winced, because he had no doubt she was livid at her father's machinations. Henry couldn't blame her father. Captain Vance had not only his daughter to protect, but a grandchild. And though Henry understood Olivia didn't want to be treated differently because she was pregnant, Henry thought an extra layer of security was a good thing. Especially because he couldn't go with her to talk to Davey Carrell. But no one had told him to stay away from Parker Wilton.

"I think it's a good idea," Henry said.

She whipped her head toward him, her eyes sparking with anger. She focused back on Gavin. "I don't need a bodyguard."

Gavin leveled an intense stare on her. "With all due respect, Lieutenant, you have become a target because of your close proximity to Detective Roarke during your investigation. No one is saying you aren't fully capable of handling yourself. Backup is to ensure everyone's safety. I trust you are close to finishing your review of the case and will be able to move on to other investigations."

Olivia pressed her lips together, presumably to keep from arguing. Finally, she nodded. "I am close to being able to present my recommendations to the review board. I have gone over the reports and interviews from my predecessor as well as my own interviews, but I have a few more questions I need answered. I'd like to interview Davey Carrell. Then I should be able to turn in my report."

"Excellent," Gavin said. "Lani will accompany you to the interview." To Henry, he said, "Training center. And you do not leave without checking in with me. Are we clear?"

Henry's stomach dropped. Tracking down Parker Wilton would have to wait. He wished he could take a moment alone with Olivia to make sure she…what? Was okay with the situation?

There was nothing okay with the situation. The faster she finished her investigation, made her recommendation and moved on to another case, the safer she would be. At least he prayed so.

With a nod at Olivia, he and Cody walked away with Noelle and Liberty. Unsure when he would see Olivia again, he couldn't quell the anxiety taking root. He lifted a prayer for her safety, even as he felt annoyance at himself for caring. Despite his best effort, his heart had grown attached to the Internal Affairs officer.

"I know you're not happy with me tagging along," Lani said as she steered her K-9 SUV through midday traffic. "I completely understand. I married to the chief of the NYC K-9 Command Unit in Queens. Doesn't exactly endear me to everyone."

Olivia sighed and reined in her frustration. "It's not you. I'm actually glad to have you with me. It wouldn't have been appropriate for Detective Roarke to accompany me to interview the person accusing him of police brutality."

Lani slanted Olivia a glance before returning her gaze to the road. "Yes, that would be a problem. You two have grown close."

Startled by the observation, Olivia's heart rate picked up. "Why do you say that?"

"Remember, I fell for my superior officer," Lani commented. "I recognize the signs. But we made it work. I transferred out."

Olivia could see herself falling for Henry if the circumstances were different. But they weren't, so entertaining ideas of a romance with the handsome detective was out of the question. Unless…she left the force. Her mind shied away from the thought.

Lani drove them through the Red Hook neighborhood of Brooklyn and Olivia pointed to one wing of a red brick, multi-story structure. "That building there."

After parking, Olivia and Lani, with Snapper trotting alongside, entered the building and found the Carrell apartment on the eighth floor.

Mrs. Carrell opened the door. She was a stout woman with dark hair that curled around her face, giving her an impish appearance. Wariness entered her dark eyes. "Can I help you?"

Olivia introduced herself and Lani, then said, "I'd like to speak with Davey."

Mrs. Carrell frowned. "Why? Our lawyer

told us not to let him talk to anyone without him present."

"I can certainly have Davey brought to a station house, if you prefer," Olivia said.

A tall young man wearing a neck brace and a cast on his left wrist walked out of the back room. "It's okay, Ma. I've got nothing to hide."

Olivia recognized Davey Carrell from the pictures taken the night of the incident.

Mrs. Carrell shook her head. "But the lawyer—"

"I've got this," Davey insisted.

Mrs. Carrell didn't appear happy but walked into the kitchen.

"What do you want to know?" Davey asked, his gaze straying to Snapper. The German shepherd's brown eyes watched the young man intently.

Olivia pulled out a pen and notepad. "Tell me what happened on the night of your injuries."

Davey recounted his version of the events that took place in Owl Head Park. His story was consistent with his statement given at the time of the incident. He'd been at the skate park and attempted to leave when Henry grabbed him, twisted his wrist until it broke and then injured his neck when Henry took him to the ground. Davey's words sounded wooden as if he rehearsed them, which Olivia supposed he had. But he couldn't maintain eye contact while giving his statement. A red flag or simply a sign of immaturity? "Do you know Parker Wilton?"

Davey stilled. "Who?"

Olivia narrowed her gaze. "You two graduated from the same high school."

Shaking his head, Davey said, "Nope. Never met him. Now, you should go or I will call my lawyer."

"Thank you for your time," Olivia said, and they left the apartment.

"He was lying," Lani stated in the hallway. "The way he shut down your questions once you mentioned Parker...he knows this Parker person."

"I agree. But the question is why lie about it unless he and Parker are working together?" Olivia filled Lani in on the information she had about Parker and his possible connection to Davey. "We need to find Parker." She glanced at the time on her phone. "He should be in class with Riley now. Do you mind a trip to Brooklyn College?"

"We're at your disposal," Lani said.

Olivia was glad to have the backup and couldn't wait to speak to Parker Wilton. Then she could put at least one part of this investigation to bed. The sooner she wrapped up, the better for everyone's sake. Including her own.

"Henry," Eden called from outside the training ring.

Dressed in a bite suit, Henry motioned to Officer Max Santelli and his K-9 partner, a black and gold rottweiler named Sam. "Give me a moment."

After training first with Noelle and Liberty, and now with Max and Sam, Henry wanted more than a moment's break, but he had his orders. Stay put and be a K-9 bite target.

Max took out a toy to play tug with Sam while Henry jogged over to Eden. The heavily padded bite suit made his gait awkward.

"What's up?" he asked.

"Lieutenant Vance wanted me to see if I could find any video footage of Parker Wilton at Owl's Head Park on the night Davey Carrell was injured," Eden told him.

Henry's gut clenched. "And?"

She shot a quick glance at Max before focusing once again on Henry. "Parker was there. I didn't know to look for him before."

Henry's heart rate doubled. "Have you told the Lieutenant?"

"I left her a voice message," Eden said. "I thought you'd want to know, also."

"I do. Thank you." But what did it mean? Parker had to be working with Davey. To what end? But how had the boys disabled his body cam that night in the park? Why the bombs, the threats and the vandalism? And how did Riley figure into their plan? What was Parker's endgame?

"Also, the lieutenant asked me to run facial recognition through various social media sites for that night, looking for anything connected to Owl's Head Park. I think I found something that might be of interest. You'll want to see this."

His curiosity piqued, Henry said, "As soon as I'm done here I'll come to your office."

"Okay, that works," she said. "I'll see you later."

Henry stood there a moment, his mind whirling. He couldn't make sense of it all. He had to find Parker Wilton. Then he would have his answers.

"Dude, you okay?" Max asked. He approached with his K-9 partner, Sam.

Sam growled, clearly ready to continue with their bite work training.

"Would you mind if we take a lunch break?"

Max shrugged. "Sure. Is everything okay with Eden?"

Henry nodded. "Yes. She's helping me on a case."

"Aren't you on modified duty?" Max said.

In lieu of an answer, he said, "I'll catch you later," and jogged out of the ring to the locker room. He made quick work of changing back into his uniform and then picked up Cody from the kennel room before going in search of his sergeant.

He found Gavin in his office and told him what he'd learned.

Gavin set aside the report he'd been reading. "Let me get this straight, you think Parker is working with Davey and trying to railroad you into the assault charges?"

"I do," Henry said.

"What proof do you have?"

"I don't have proof. Just my gut feeling. I need to talk to Parker. He's involved my sister."

"How?"

"By trying to date her and not leaving her alone when she refused. I want to find out why."

Gavin contemplated the request. "Hmm. You can't compromise the Carrell case."

"I won't," Henry promised. "I'll just ask the kid what his intentions are toward Riley."

"Not alone. Take someone with you. Feel

the kid out, but don't make any references to Davey Carrell."

"Thanks, Sarge." Henry backed out of the office. If his boss had noticed that Henry hadn't promised not to dig into the connection between Parker and Davey, he didn't call him on it.

He went in search of Bradley but instead found Olivia and Lani entering the building.

"Parker was at Owl's Head Park the night of the incident with Davey Carrell," Henry said, without preamble.

"We're convinced Davey knows Parker," Olivia said at the same time.

Henry digested her words. "He does?"

Olivia nodded. "Yes, though he lied to me about it. Parker was there? That's interesting. And unlikely a coincidence."

"I'm on my way to talk to Parker," Henry said.

"He didn't show up at the college today," Olivia told him. "We stopped by there on the way back."

"I'll go to his house," Henry said. "Do you want to come?"

"Of course," she said.

A throat clearing brought their attention to Lani. "I'll drive. Someone has to keep you two out of trouble."

THIRTEEN

While Lani drove the large SUV with the dogs in separate crates in the back, Henry sat in the front passenger seat willing her to drive faster. He had to find out what Parker and Davey were up to, and how Riley figured into their plan. Olivia sat forward in the back passenger seat. He appreciated her calming presence.

She didn't have to be here. Undoubtedly shouldn't be, but he was loathe to do this without her.

In a short amount of time he'd come to respect and admire the woman. His feelings ran deeper but he couldn't let himself acknowledge them. Because if he did, he didn't know how he'd ever be able to walk away.

Right now he needed to stay focused on

finding out if Parker Wilton was the bombing suspect. And what the kid wanted from Riley. That had to be his priority.

Once again entering the peninsula village of Red Hook, Lani found a parking spot near the five-story walk-up where Parker and his mother, Karen, lived.

"Snapper and I will keep watch outside," Lani said as Henry popped open his door.

"If you see anything suspicious let us know and call for more backup," Henry told her.

"Will do."

He hurried around to the back of the SUV to release Cody.

"We don't want to go in there making any accusations," Olivia warned as they walked into the building.

"I'll try to keep my accusations to a minimum," Henry said. "But I can't promise."

She stopped him on the landing of the fourth floor. "Henry, you let me do the talking."

He liked her all fierce and serious. She was a woman of substance with a strong will and a sharp mind. He wished the circumstances were different. "I will do my best."

Giving him a stern look, she said, "I hope so."

They approached the door. Henry let Cody sniff the edges but showed no sign of an alert. Henry rapped his knuckles sharply on the door.

After a moment, the door opened to reveal a petite woman holding a coffee mug and wearing the waitressing uniform of a local chain restaurant. Her light brown eyes widened. "Yes?"

"Are you Mrs. Wilton?" Olivia stepped forward with her badge in hand.

"That's right. It's actually Miss. But Karen is fine. Can I help you, officers?" She tilted her head as she gazed at Henry.

"I'm Lieutenant Vance and this is Detective Roarke with the Brooklyn K-9 Unit. May we come in?"

Karen stepped aside and opened the door wider for them to enter. The apartment was small but well kept. There were pictures of Parker on the walls, mostly school photos.

Setting her mug on the kitchen counter, Karen stared at Henry. "I remember you."

Henry was sure he'd never seen the woman before or been to this apartment. "I'm sorry?"

Karen smiled. "I know you don't recognize me. I'm not surprised. I looked very different the last time we met."

"Okay." Henry searched his memory for some recollection of this woman and came up blank. "Can you remind me?"

"Six years ago, you saved my life. And my son's."

Memories surged and Henry's heart twisted in his chest. He exchanged a glance with Olivia. This was the woman from the domestic case that Olivia had questioned him about. Her husband had accused Henry of excessive force.

"I do remember," Henry said. "But you had a different last name."

"Yes," she affirmed. "When I recovered from the abuse, I filed for divorce and took back my maiden name. And I changed my son's last name, also."

"I'm glad to know you recovered and got out of that situation," Henry said with sincerity. "Whatever happened to your husband?" Could her ex-husband be behind the bombings? Had he attacked Olivia in the museum?

"Jack died in prison."

Henry wasn't sure what to say. He wanted to offer condolences, but the words stuck in his throat. He wasn't happy that a life was lost but the man *had* beaten his wife nearly to death. It was hard to find sympathy but he dredged up what he could. "I'm sure the loss was hard for you and your son."

Karen's lips twisted. "Yes. For Parker, anyway."

Henry had a bad feeling about Parker Wilton's state of mind. "Is your son home?"

Olivia shot him a censuring glance. "We have some questions for Parker."

Karen shook her head. "Parker has an apartment with some other kids his age. I haven't been there yet. I work swing shift at the restaurant. It leaves little time for socializing."

Cody sniffed the floor and sat in front of a closed door.

Henry moved to the door. "What's in here?"

"Coats."

"Can you open it, please?" Olivia asked.

Clearly confused, Karen went to the door and pulled it open. Coats hung on hangers, shoes lined the floor. Cody moved forward to sniff and sat in front of a pair of athletic shoes. "Are these Parker's?" Henry asked.

"Yes, those are. Why is your dog sniffing his shoes?"

"Does Parker have a room here?" Olivia moved toward the hallway.

"He does." Karen hurried to catch up with her. "In case he ever wants to come home."

"May we see it?" Olivia's words were polite, but Henry heard the tension in her tone.

"Why do you need to see his room? He's not here. What is going on?"

Olivia faced the woman. "I'm sorry to tell

you this, but your son is a person of interest in the case we're working."

Karen seemed to deflate. "What has he done?"

"We're in the early stages of the investigation and his name came up," Olivia said. "I'd rather not accuse him of something without proof."

Karen scoffed. "I've tried everything I can to keep him on the straight and narrow. He just seems to want to follow in his father's footsteps." She walked forward and opened a door. "This is his room."

Henry crowded past the women to enter Parker's personal space. It was neat and tidy. Posters of sports icons decorated the walls. The bed was made with a simple blue comforter and a desk that looked like it had never been used stood under the window. Cody sniffed around the room but didn't alert.

"Do you have the address where Parker's staying?" Henry asked.

Karen grabbed a piece of paper and a pen from the desk and wrote down an address. "You can probably find him at work. He's been working at the Tire Mart over in Gowanus since he was sixteen. That's how he can afford to live on his own."

"I took my SUV there last March when I had a nail in the back tire," Henry said to Olivia.

Her eyes widened with understanding. She turned to Karen. "Does Parker drive a silver sedan?"

"Sometimes." Karen walked back into the living room. Henry, Cody and Olivia followed. "His boss has a bunch of different cars that he allows his employees to use. He's been very generous with Parker."

"Do you know a young man named Davey Carrell?" Olivia asked.

Karen tilted her head. "The name does sound familiar. Does he work with Parker?"

"Not that we know of," Olivia said. "But they may have gone to high school together."

"Oh." Karen held up a hand. "Just a moment." She left the room.

Olivia grabbed Henry's arm. "Do you

think Parker blames you for his father's death?"

He'd had that same thought. "Possibly. But why pursue Riley?"

Before Olivia could speculate, Karen returned with a yearbook in hand. She flipped through the pages until she found one that had a group photo. "Okay, here you go. Davey and Parker were classmates. They both were part of the technology club."

Henry stared at the photo of the boys sitting together at a table working on electronics. "Do you mind if I look through this?"

"Not at all," Karen said.

Henry flipped through the book. Olivia pressed close to him to see the pages. Her fresh apple scent was distracting and reminded him of her sweet kiss.

Henry flipped the page to the formal senior photos and froze. Beneath Parker's image the caption read, *Oh, yeah! Life is really great. LOLZ.*

Henry shivered. LOLZ! Just like in the texts. Parker had to be the bomber.

Meeting Olivia's gaze, Henry could see

she agreed by the grim expression in her eyes. She turned to Karen. "Do you mind if we take this?"

"Sure. How much trouble is Parker in?"

"It's hard to say at this moment, but we believe he's been targeting Detective Roarke and those close to him," Olivia said.

Karen's dropped her head into her hands. "This is his dad's fault." She lifted her head. "Jack sent Parker letters. I found them after the fact. They were full of hate for the police." She gave Henry an apologetic look. "And you specifically."

"But from what I understand, Detective Roarke saved you and your son that night," Olivia said. "Doesn't Parker remember that?"

Karen shook her head. "No. The counselor I took him to said he has dissociative amnesia. He remembers only the good times with his father. Parker has no memory of the abuse or the months in foster care while I recovered in the hospital."

"Selective memory loss?" Henry said. He looked at Olivia. "Is that a thing?"

"Yes, and needs to be taken quite seriously," she replied. "It stems from the effects of extreme stress as a part of post-traumatic stress disorder."

Henry mulled that over. The kid was experiencing PTSD. But that didn't excuse what he'd done so far. Nor explain why he was pushing Riley to date him.

Olivia handed Karen a card. "If you hear from Parker or he comes home, please call me. I really need to speak with him."

"Detective Roarke," Karen said when they were at the door, ready to leave. "I never got to say thank you. I'm not kidding when I say you saved my life. The doctor said if you and your partner hadn't arrived when you had and pulled Jack off me, I would've died. And I don't know what would've happened to Parker if you hadn't intervened."

Henry nodded, appreciating her words. He'd done his job that day. As he did every day. Protecting and serving the citizens of New York was the creed that got him through the worst days of his life. "I'm glad I was able to help you."

Sadness washed over him to think her son was now going to be the one in trouble.

Lani was waiting in the vehicle at the curb. After securing Cody in the crate at the back of the SUV, Henry climbed in the front passenger seat. "Any problems?"

"No," she said. "Did you get what you were hoping for here?"

Olivia filled Lani in as she drove. "Davey *did* lie to us. I'll be seeing him again, but next time in an interrogation room. But for now, I think we need to pay a visit to the Tire Mart. You okay with that, Lani?"

"Sure."

Olivia gave her the address. The SUV merged into traffic, headed for the neighborhood of Gowanus.

"I've been here," Henry said as Lani pulled up to the garage that took up the whole block. He told them about the nail in his tire. "That must be why Parker seemed familiar to me. He wasn't nearly as tall or filled out at age thirteen as he is now at nineteen, so I didn't connect him to the domestic violence case from six years ago. He must've worked on the SUV."

"And the sight of you must have brought back all of his rage and given him someone to blame, starting him on his quest for revenge," Olivia said. "Lani, you good to join us? I'm not sure how Parker will respond."

"That's what I'm here for." Lani unbuckled and hopped out.

After releasing the dogs, Henry led the way inside. The garage had large bays, with cars being worked on by men of a wide range of ages. But Henry didn't see Parker.

"We're looking for the owner," Henry called out.

"He's in his office," a man said, pointing to a glass-walled enclosure.

A man in his late sixties with a full head of shocking white hair and bright blue eyes opened his office door and motioned them in. "Morton Daniels at your service. To what do I owe this visit?"

"We're looking for Parker Wilton," Olivia said. "We understand he works here."

"Parker hasn't shown up for the past two days. He's usually not flaky," Morton said.

"We understand that you have a silver sedan that you let your employees borrow," Olivia said. "Is it here?"

"Should be parked out in the lot." They walked out of the tire center and into the back where there were five or six different kinds of cars parked. But no silver sedan. "Somebody must have it out. Let me check the logbook."

They followed him back to his office. "Hmm. Last person to check out the silver sedan was Parker. It doesn't show it coming back in." The man shook his head. "I assume since you're looking for him he's in some sort of trouble. I feel bad for his mama. She's nice."

Olivia handed the man her card. "If Parker returns, can you please call me?"

"Will do, ma'am," Morton said, taking the card and tucking it into the pocket of his work shirt.

Once they were headed back to the station, Olivia said, "This puts a different spin on things. Once we find Parker and interview him, I have a feeling we'll know for sure if you're being set up for Davey Carrell's injuries."

"Which reminds me," Henry said. "Eden found something that she thought we might be interested in seeing."

As soon as they were back at the station they went to Eden's office, but she'd left for the evening.

"We'll have to catch her tomorrow," Henry said.

"Isn't the Colt Colton concert tomorrow night?" Olivia asked.

Henry groaned. "Yes, it is. I can't let Riley go to that concert. Not until I know Parker's in custody."

"The venue has tight security with bag checks and wand detectors," Olivia said slowly. "We can alert them to be extra vigilant. And if...we accompany her, she'll be safe."

Henry blinked in surprise. He was pleased by the suggestion but not sure he should take her up on the offer. "Really?"

"Yes, really."

"Riley will be thrilled. But we'll have to clear it with the brass." Henry wouldn't admit it aloud but he was thrilled, as well. Though he was afraid spending more time with Olivia outside of work wasn't the best idea. But then again, he was an innocent man being wrongly accused, just as he'd maintained from the beginning. And if they could prove his innocence, then there would be no issue of impropriety, right? Spending more time with her was a risk, not only because she was investigating him, but his feeling for her were growing. Changing. Would it be so bad if he fell in love with Olivia? Yes it would. As long as she was IA and he part of the rank and file, they could never be together.

The next morning when Henry informed Riley of the plan, he'd been right, she was thrilled to hear that not only would she be allowed to go, but that Olivia and Henry would be going to the concert, as well. Gavin, after discussing the situation with

Olivia's boss, had given them the green light. Apparently Olivia had made the case that she needed to be in attendance to observe how Henry reacted in a crowded, stressful situation.

"But you're not sitting near me?" Riley asked. "Right?"

"No, we won't sit near you," Henry assured her. But he would sit where he could keep an eye on her. Because they still hadn't found Parker, even with every patrol officer on the lookout for the bombing suspect and the silver sedan. It had been a long, worrisome night, but Parker hadn't surfaced. Henry speculated that maybe he had skipped town.

"After school, I'm going to get ready for the concert at Kelsey's. You can pick us up there." Riley put her backpack on.

"Why can't Kelsey come here?"

"Because we've already decided we're meeting at her house."

"Officer Hall will escort you to school and to Kelsey's. You don't leave her apartment until I get there," Henry said. "Understand?"

"Yes, I understand. I'm not going to do anything foolish," Riley said. Her gaze narrowed. "Henry, I really like Olivia. I think she's good for you."

Henry gathered Riley in his arms and hugged her close. "I like her, too. But I can't do anything about it because of our jobs."

Hugging him back, Riley said, "Some things are more important. Don't let her get away. She's a good catch."

Riley's words echoed through his brain. Olivia was a woman worth loving. His heart was well on its way there. And despite his assertions that he didn't want to be a parent, he wanted to be a part of her and her child's life. How out-there was that? Especially when there was no way it could happen while he was suspected of using excessive force.

Mind whirling in directions he had no business going, Henry and Cody walked Riley out to the curb where Officer Hall sat in an unmarked cruiser. He'd been assigned to drive Riley to and from school until the bomber was caught.

"Be safe," he said before shutting door. He watched the car drive away and he lifted up a prayer to God for her protection.

A few minutes later, Bradley McGregor arrived in his K-9 unit vehicle. "Heard you needed a ride."

"That I do, my friend." Lifting Cody into his arms, Henry climbed in and they headed to work. And then tonight he'd be going to the concert with Olivia. If only this wasn't a potentially dangerous situation.

Because Lani and Snapper had been called away on a pressing matter, Henry had volunteered to use one of the K9 unit's other vehicles to drive Olivia to her late morning appointment. There was a look of consternation on his face when she told him the visit was to her ob-gyn for a checkup. She quickly apologized. "I'm sorry you're having to accompany me here. I should have taken a taxi."

He frowned as he pulled the vehicle to the

curb. "No, it's fine. I want you to be fine. I'm happy to do this for you."

"After all the stress and drama of the past few days, I want to be sure all is well with the pregnancy."

"Of course," Henry said as he tugged at the collar of his uniform. "Is it okay if I wait here?"

She laughed. "Yes. You don't have to come inside. That would be awkward."

Relief swept over his face. "Okay. If you need anything, call me. I'll come running."

Touched by his words, she nodded and hurried inside the building. She didn't have to wait long to be seen.

"You and the baby are both healthy and strong," Doctor Smooter said as she moved the ultrasound probe over Olivia's belly. "Are you still wanting to be surprised by the gender?"

Olivia nodded. "Yes. I think I'll need that to look forward to when the time to have this baby comes." The delivery part of being pregnant was overwhelming to think about, though her mother and sister-in-law had assured her she'd get through it just fine.

"All right." Doctor Smooter pressed a button and an image printed. After cleaning the ultrasound gel off of her abdomen and allowing Olivia to get dressed, the doctor handed her the sonogram print of her baby. "We'll see you next month."

Taking the image with her, Olivia's heart swelled with love for the tiny person inside of her.

"Everything okay?" Henry asked once Olivia was seated in the passenger seat of the SUV.

"All good." She held up the square sheet showing the shadowy image outlining her baby's form. "It's so amazing to think soon I'll be a mother."

"You already are," Henry commented.

Right. Excitement revved through her system and her mind jumped ahead to what she would do once the baby came. Would she stay with the force? The question was one Olivia had asked herself multiple times. As single mother, she'd need an income. And her family had offered to help with childcare.

She still had several months to decide what she wanted for her and her baby's future. She prayed that God would reveal to her the right decision to make.

However, at the moment, she needed to concentrate on proving Henry was innocent of the charges leveled against him. She needed to crack Davey Carrell's story. For Henry's sake. She wanted to repay him for all his kindness to her. And her heart whispered there were other reasons, like she was falling for him, was something she had to ignore.

Later that afternoon, Henry sat in Gavin's office going over the particulars of what he and Olivia had gathered so far about Davey Carrell and Parker Wilton. Cody sat at his feet while Gavin's dog, Tommy, a brown and white springer spaniel, lay curled on the bed in the corner.

After seeing the sonogram image of Olivia's baby, Henry couldn't help but be excited for her. The image made the baby real. And stirred in him a yearning he hadn't expected. What would it be like to be a father from the beginning?

The familiar chime of the incoming text sounded, cutting off his thoughts as dread gripped Henry's insides.

Roses are red, violets are blue, concerts are the perfect place for kaaaaboom! LOLZ

Jumping to his feet, Henry read the text to Gavin. There were still two hours before the concert started. The doors would be opening soon. "It has to be Parker. We have to go to the concert hall now and secure the bomb before they let people in."

"Agreed." Gavin rose and retrieved his sidearm from the bottom desk drawer. "You ride with me and Tommy."

The sergeant made calls as they hustled to Gavin's vehicle.

On the way to the Barclays Center, Henry called Olivia. "We just got a bomb threat at the concert arena. We are on our way there now," he told her. "Can you go and secure my sister? I know Officer Hall is there, but I just want to be sure that she's okay."

Olivia promised she and Lani would go directly to Kelsey's apartment, giving Henry a measure of peace. The concert wasn't for several more hours and Henry was grateful Parker was giving him notice. But the arena was massive. Home to the Brooklyn Nets basketball team and the New York Islanders of the National Hockey League, the Barclays Center had over nineteen thousand seats and a hundred and one suites, not to mention the many eateries within its glass and metal structure. It would take hours for them to find an explosive device even with their highly trained dogs.

Gavin alerted the center's security and then called for more bomb-sniffing dogs from all five boroughs and the explosive ordnance disposal specialists to convene at the center.

When they arrived at the Barclays Center, sirens blazing, Gavin organized the search. He had the officers spread out. With worry eating at his gut, Henry and Cody worked methodically, checking row after row of seats.

They had to find the bomb before it was too late. And he thanked God Riley and Olivia and the baby were nowhere near the center.

Olivia tried calling Riley's cell phone, but it went directly to voice mail. "Riley, call me. I'm on my way to Kelsey's now."

Trying not to be overly worried by the lack of response, Olivia willed the traffic to lighten up as Lani drove to the address Henry had given for Kelsey's apartment in Brooklyn Heights.

When they arrived and parked, Olivia noted Officer Hall's empty car at the curb. Telling herself Riley's phone was buried in her backpack and she couldn't hear it ringing, Olivia and Lani and the German shepherd, Snapper, hurried into the building. The elevator had an "out of service" note taped to the door.

"The stairs," Olivia said as she veered to

the stairwell. She made quick work of the five flights of stairs, then moved quickly to apartment 5D and knocked.

The door was jerked open by Riley's friend Kelsey. Olivia recognized the petite girl from Coney Island. "Hi, Kelsey. I need to speak with Riley."

Worry clouded Kelsey's dark eyes. "She hasn't shown up yet. I've been calling her cell, but she doesn't answer."

Olivia's heart pumped with dread. Where could Riley be? Where was Officer Hall? "If you hear from her, tell her to call Olivia."

"We have to find her," Olivia said to Lani as they retraced their steps to the first floor.

"I'll call Eden and ask her to ping Hall's phone," Lani said.

"Good idea. I have to call Henry and let him know."

They headed for the exit, but Olivia heard a phone ringing. "It's coming from the elevator."

She hurried over to the closed elevator doors and banged on them. "Hello! Is somebody in there?"

Snapper barked and scratched at the metal doors.

There was a moan.

"Somebody's stuck inside the elevator," Olivia said.

Together they pried the elevator doors open and found Officer Hall lying on the floor, holding his bleeding head.

"What happened?" Olivia asked. "Where's Riley?"

"Riley and I were headed into the elevator when something struck me from behind. I went down like a house of cards. I blacked out." He grimaced. "I don't know who took her."

Olivia stomach sank.

Riley had been kidnapped!

FOURTEEN

Henry's phone rang, the sound echoing across the cavernous Barclays Center and setting his already tightly strung nerves on edge. He and Cody were near the stage that had been set up for the concert. The large speakers and lighting equipment above and to the sides of the stage would make excellent hiding places for explosive devices.

Henry hadn't figured out exactly how Parker had managed to plant a bomb in the highly secure facility. But the priority was to find it.

He dug his phone out of his pocket and checked the caller ID. Olivia.

Just seeing her name on the small screen sent a burst of warmth through him. He answered with, "Hey, have you secured Riley?"

There was a moment of hesitation that sent his senses on alert. A chill whispered across his nape.

"No. Henry, she's gone," Olivia's voice shook.

Dread had a feral grip on his lungs. "What do you mean, 'gone'?"

"Kidnapped. Somebody knocked out Officer Hall, and Riley's nowhere to be found."

Horror flooded Henry's veins. His sister was in trouble. Possibly hurt. How would he survive another death of someone he loved?

With a quick tug on Cody's leash, he and the dog ran toward the exit doors of the Barclays Center as he spoke. "Parker did this. We have to find him before he does something to my sister!"

"I'm going back to talk to Parker's mother. I'll see if she can come up with any idea where her son might have taken Riley," Olivia said, her voice stronger.

"His mom doesn't have the address of where he's been staying. But maybe those people at the Tire Mart do," Henry said. "I'm headed there now."

"What about the bomb threat at Barclays?"

"I trust the others will find it," he told her. "Be careful. Parker may have returned to his mother's. If so, call for back up."

"I will," she assured him. "You do the same. Don't be a hero. Riley can't lose you."

He needed to find Riley. To save his sister.

He and Cody ran outside and skidded to a halt. He didn't have a vehicle here. He'd come with Gavin. He whirled around and raced back inside. He found his boss talking with the center's management.

"Excuse me," Henry said as he interrupted. "I need the keys to the SUV. Riley is missing. I need to go find her."

"We'll go with you," Gavin said without hesitation.

They ran out the door to the K-9 vehicle parked at an angle at the curb. Instead of just calling to see if Parker was at the garage, Henry gave Gavin the address of the Tire Mart. He needed to make sure Parker didn't have Riley hidden in a room there. Sirens blaring, they raced toward the Gowanus neighborhood, weaving in and out of the evening traffic.

Leaning forward with a hand on the dashboard, Henry willed the vehicle to go faster and lifted fervent prayers to God to keep his sister safe. It was late in the day and traffic was heavy. By the time they reached the Tire Mart, anxiety had a stranglehold on his insides.

Everything hurt, but mostly his heart. Gavin had barely stopped the SUV when Henry leapt out and raced inside the garage, Cody at his heels. While Gavin and his K-9 did a search of the premises for Riley and Parker, Henry found the owner, Morton Daniels, in the vehicle bay. "We need an address for Parker Wilton now."

Raising his bushy white eyebrows, Morton said, "This way. I think I might have one." He led them to his office. He flipped through some files and pulled out an address. "This is the only address I have for Parker."

It was for Parker's mother's apartment. Frustration tightened the knots in Henry's shoulder muscles. "No, he's staying somewhere else. Maybe with some of the guys here. I need to question them."

Gavin came up behind them. "We checked the entire garage. Parker doesn't have her here." He looked at Henry. "Slow down. You're not going to help your sister by charging all over the place. Be methodical and go by the book."

Forcing himself to take measured breaths, Henry nodded. He walked at a fast clip to the garage bay where several men worked on the lift-raised cars. Henry gave a sharp whistle to gain their attention. "I need to find Parker Wilton, now. If anybody has any information about where he's staying or where he'd go, I need you to come forward. This is a matter of life and death."

Back in the far corner an argument broke out between a couple of guys. One pushed the other into a stack of tires, causing the tires to fall and bounce all over, drawing everyone's attention.

Henry hurried over to the two young men. "What do you know?" Cody sniffed both of the kids and then turned his attention to the tires but soon lost interest there, as well.

The two young men, both in their early twenties, looked at each other.

"You're not in trouble," Henry assured them.

One shrugged and said, "Parker's been staying with us. We needed more roommates to make the rent."

"We need the address," Gavin said.

One of them rattled off a street address in Red Hook.

"Thank you." Leading Cody back to the SUV, Henry called Olivia as Gavin climbed behind the wheel. He gave her the address of where Riley might be.

"That's not far from where we are," Olivia told him.

The last thing he wanted was for Olivia and her baby to be in danger, too. He would never forgive himself if something happened to either of them. "Promise me you'll wait for me to get there."

"We don't have time to wait," she said. "Lani and I are on it."

He had no say in her actions but he couldn't help the ache in his chest. "Please, be careful."

After securing Cody in the back beside Tommy, Henry urged Gavin to drive faster through the commuter traffic.

Please, Lord, please, let me get there in time to help Lani and Olivia save my sister.

Before Lani had brought the SUV to a full stop at the curb in front of the apartment building, Olivia jumped out. Her heart beat in her throat and dread made her queasy. The red brick building looked like every other building on the block. But this one held Riley. She was sure of it.

Olivia ran up to the entrance.

"Lieutenant, wait," Lani called as she released Snapper from the back of the SUV.

Seconds ticking away, Olivia's skin crawled with urgency. Lani and Snapper joined her at the door. Olivia hesitated. Was the door rigged to explode? There was no reason for her to believe Parker would wire an explosive to the entrance to his own building. She reached for the door handle and rattled it. Locked. She pounded her fist against the door.

Lani put her hand on Olivia's arm. "We need to take this slow. We don't want to spook him."

Dropping her hand to her side, Olivia took shallow breaths. For a moment the world spun, then righted itself. "Of course. But what if he's hurt her?" The thought filled Olivia with an anguish so deep she thought she might be sick.

"We can't think that way."

"I'm not cut out for this," Olivia said.

She'd never enjoyed patrol, but this was worse than anything she'd faced. The unknown, the threat to someone she loved. It was one thing to investigate, following facts and making recommendations, but being out in the field like this was nerve-racking. Why had she ever thought that going into law enforcement was the right decision? Because everyone else in her family had, that was why.

Shaking off the self-doubt, she put a hand over her belly. She needed to stay calm for the child she carried. For Riley and Henry. But how could she remain calm when her heart was torn up thinking that something might happen to Riley? Henry wouldn't be able to survive if his sister were hurt. Olivia's heart throbbed.

Lani started buzzing all the apartments on the call box to the left of the door, until finally someone answered the call.

"Yeah, what you want?" a male voice said through the crackle of static from the box on the wall.

"Police. We need to get into the building. Possible bomb threat," Lani said.

"What?" the man screeched.

"Please unlock the door and leave the building," Lani said.

The door unlocked.

Olivia paused in the entryway, torn between her desire to charge forward and her need to keep civilians safe. "We should evacuate everyone."

"I'll find the building superintendent and have him go floor by floor to empty the building," Lani said.

Thankful to Lani for her levelheadedness, Olivia nodded. "I'll take the elevator to the sixth floor and start the evacuation process there before we approach 6C."

With effort, Olivia remained calm as she raced to the elevator. She checked her service weapon holstered at her back. She'd never fired it in the line of duty. And she hoped today wouldn't be the first time. Regardless, she unholstered the weapon, keeping it at the ready in two hands as the elevator rumbled upward. She stepped out of onto the sixth floor and took a moment to orient herself.

Apartment 6C was at the end of the hall. The stairwell door opened behind her. She spun, her body tensing.

Lani and Snapper jogged toward her. Olivia let out a breath of relief and lowered her weapon.

"I found the building superintendent. He's evacuating the lower floors," Lani said.

"Let's get this floor emptied," Olivia instructed. They knocked on doors and urged people to quietly leave the building. Finally, Olivia and Lani approached apartment 6C.

Lani rapped her knuckles on the door.

For a long moment, no one answered. They could hear noises coming from inside the apartment. A faint scream. A slammed door.

"That sounds like probable cause to me," Lani said. "You good with that, Lieutenant?"

"I sure am," Olivia said.

Lani motioned Olivia back, then she raised her right foot and kicked in the door.

Parker Wilton ran out from a back room, slamming the door behind him. Snapper barked and growled at him.

Olivia and Lani both trained their weapons at the threat. Parker skidded to halt and shoved his hands into his sweatshirt pockets.

"Hands up!" Lani shouted.

Not complying, Parker backed away from the snarling dog and looked past the two officers. "Where's Roarke?"

"Get your hands where we can see them!" Olivia commanded.

Parker stared at her for a moment, then lifted his hands with the fingers of his right hand curled around what appeared to be a detonator, his thumb hovering over the trigger. "Do you know what this is?" he taunted. "A detonator. Works like a cell phone. I push this button, it connects wirelessly to a bomb and the whole building goes up in smoke." He looked at Lani. "Call off your dog."

"Heel." Lani gave the sharp command and Snapper returned to her side but stayed standing, ears back and tail high.

Olivia forced air into her tight lungs. "Where's Riley?"

"She's fine." He pointed to the exit. "You need to leave."

"Not without Riley. Have you hurt her?" Olivia's voice rose and she inwardly grimaced. It wouldn't help to panic now.

Parker stared at Olivia as if she had grown

a third eye. "She's okay. I would never hurt her. I love her."

Stunned by the admission, Olivia tried to make sense of his actions. "Why kidnap her? Why have you been taunting her brother and hurting people?"

Olivia heard a thump from inside the room that Parker had just exited. Olivia held up her hands. "Parker, I'm setting my weapon down." Slowly, she set her sidearm on the ground and kicked it backward toward Lani. "I'm not a threat to you. Let me see Riley." She moved cautiously toward the door, skirting around Parker.

Parker spun and grabbed Olivia by the back of the neck, opened the door and pushed her inside. He followed, slamming the door behind him and twisting the lock. Then he pushed a nightstand in front of the door.

Snapper battered the door, scratching and barking.

"Lieutenant Vance!" Lani's cry penetrated the room.

Stunned, Olivia caught her breath. "I'm okay."

Riley was nowhere in sight. Olivia stared at the photos of Henry plastered all over the walls with big Xs drawn over them with red marker. There were photos of Riley, as well. But her pictures were grouped together in the shape of a heart. Parker had been stalking the siblings for very different reasons.

Olivia faced Parker. "You haven't killed anyone yet. Everything you've done so far has been fairly minor," she said. "You need to surrender yourself, now. Before this gets to a point where there's no turning back."

Something thumped from within the closet, drawing Olivia's attention. She lunged for the door, but Parker was faster. He grabbed Olivia, pushing her down onto a chair that had been fitted with an explosive device made with wires and a cell phone.

Olivia's heart nearly stuttered to a stop. The door shook as Lani tried to kick it open.

"Officer Jameson, I'm sitting on a bomb. Stand down," Olivia yelled as fear sliced like an open wound through her. Focusing her energy on Parker, Olivia kept her tone calm. "Parker, what are you doing? Where's Riley?"

The thump came from the closet again. Parker growled and then yanked the door open. Riley sat on the floor, hands bound and black tape over her mouth. She kicked at Parker, but he scuttled backward.

"She's a feisty one," he said. "But that's good. We're gonna run off together. I have to save her from her brother. He's a bully. He makes life hard for her. But once he's dead, she'll be all mine."

Anxiety twisted within Olivia's chest. Remembering what his mother had said about his dissociative amnesia, Olivia wanted to gauge his mental state. "Why do you want to hurt Henry?"

"He put my dad in prison. He deserves to die. He took my father away. Because of him, my dad is dead. If it weren't for Detective Roarke, my mom and dad would still be married and we'd be one big happy family."

"Parker, I talked to your mother," Olivia said in an even, nonthreatening tone. "You don't remember the night your father was taken away."

"I do remember," he insisted. "I remember that officer punching my dad and then throwing him into the car. There was no reason for him to do that. He had no right to take my father from me and my mom."

"Henry saved your mother's life that night, Parker. And your life, as well," Olivia said.

"No, he ruined my life." Parker paced in front of Olivia. "He ruined everything."

"Parker, your mother was badly beaten that night. And it hadn't been the first time. Your father was going to hurt you, too."

"No!" Parker stopped and rubbed at his head as if his brain was hurting him. He was still holding the detonator.

Maybe the memories were coming back. At least Olivia hoped so. She needed to keep reminding him of the truth. Keep him talking so he wouldn't do anything drastic. "Your mother was put in the hospital for a long time. Do you remember? You were in foster care. Your dad did that to your mother. He nearly killed her."

"It didn't happen." Parker pounded his forehead with his empty hand. "You're making that up."

Afraid she was pushing too hard, she changed tactics. "Parker, listen to me. You don't want to hurt Riley. You love her. She's a nice girl. So just let us go."

Parker froze. His gaze jumped to Riley sitting on the floor of the closet. "No. If she'd only gone out with me, things wouldn't be like this."

Riley whimpered.

Shaking her head, hoping Riley would understand, Olivia said, "This isn't Riley's fault. And it's not Henry's fault. You targeted Riley to get close to her brother, right?"

"That's how it started," he said. "Then I really started to like her."

"What's your plan?" Olivia pressed. "How will you and Riley live?"

Parker grabbed a duffel bag from the bed. "I've got money. I've been saving. We'll be fine."

He wouldn't get out of the city. And Riley

could get hurt in the process. "Did you plant a bomb at Barclays Center?"

Lips twisting, Parker said, "Naw. I just needed Roarke and his dog out of the way."

Which left Riley vulnerable with an officer who wasn't expecting an ambush. "How did you get Henry's personal cell phone number?"

Parker shrugged. "That was easy." He used his thumb to point at Riley. "She left her phone out one day in class. Unlocked."

He squatted down by Riley and caressed her cheek. She pulled away from him and he grabbed a handful of her hair. "So pretty."

With his back turned away from her, Olivia inched off the chair. If she could tackle him and secure the hand that held the detonator, then she could call to Lani. The officer could break the door in and arrest Parker.

In a swift move, Parker jumped to his feet and closed the distance between them in two long strides. He pushed Olivia back down on to the chair. "Oh no, you don't!" he yelled. "You're gonna stay right there."

Parker grabbed Riley by the biceps and pulled her to her feet. His dark eyes were malicious as he stared at Olivia. "You get off that chair again and I push this." He waved the detonator at her. "And then we all die."

Olivia shared a panicked glance with the younger woman. "You don't want to do that. You don't want to hurt Riley, remember?"

Olivia could hear Lani talking on the other side of the door, then muted male voices answering. Olivia recognized Henry's deep timbre. Hope blossomed in her chest. And yet she was afraid Henry's presence might push Parker over the edge. She needed to keep Parker distracted. "What about Davey?"

"What about him?" Parker said, seemingly oblivious to the voices outside the bedroom door.

"How did the two of you disable Detective Roarke's body camera at Owl's Head Park?"

"That was easy," Parker said. "An EMP. Any dummy could do it."

The unit's technology expert had said an electromagnet could have interfered with the feed. Apparently Parker had built himself an electromagnetic pulse device. "No," Olivia countered. "You're smart, Parker. Smarter than most. You know there's no way you're leaving here with Riley."

A sudden pounding on the door jolted through Olivia. Parker whipped around and stared at the door.

"Parker Wilton, this is Sergeant Gavin Sutherland of the Brooklyn K-9 Unit. Open this door so we can talk," Gavin called through the door.

"You don't get to give me orders," Parker yelled back. He pulled Riley in front of him. "Where's Roarke?"

"I'm here," came Henry's reply. "Are the lieutenant and my sister okay?"

"Henry, we're okay for now," Olivia called to him. "Parker has a detonator in his hand and there's a bomb in here. No explosives at Barclays Center, according to Parker."

"Now who's in control?" Parker yelled. "How do you like it? You made my father go to prison. Now Riley is mine. You took what I love, now I'm taking what you love."

"Listen, buddy," Henry said, his voice calm. "Why don't you open the door and come out. Everyone's going to the concert tonight. Colt Colton. It should be a great time. You could sit with Riley and her friends. There's an extra seat since one of the girls can't make it."

Parker's expression changed, revealing the young soul inside him. "Really?"

Olivia could tell he was excited by the idea. He really was a troubled young man.

Then he scowled, looking at Riley. "You think I'm dumb. The minute I open that door, you're going to arrest me and take Riley away from me. She's mine now. And you better step back, because I'm coming out with her." He pushed Riley toward the door. "But if you do anything at all, I hit the button and everyone goes kaboom."

FIFTEEN

Olivia's heart pounded in her chest, her pulse roared in her ears. She had to stall, do something to keep the troubled young man from imploding and blowing them all sky high. "Parker, why did you try to break into Henry and Riley's condo?"

Parker paused and pointed at the simple gold cross hanging around Riley's neck. "I was hoping I could take that. And then, if she thought she'd lost it and I found it, she'd see I wasn't such a bad guy." His face twisted with rage. "But he stopped me. Him and that dog."

"Why were you following him? You've been doing that for months. Did you recognize him when he brought his vehicle into the Tire Mart?"

"I recognized the name. My dad would write to me. And he'd tell me that an officer named Roarke was the one who put him in jail. That Roarke was the reason we couldn't be together. That Roarke broke up our family."

"You know that's not true." Compassion flooded Olivia. This boy, with his trauma-induced faulty memory, had been brainwashed by an abusive, manipulative father. Parker needed to remember what actually happened so that the truth could release him from this prison of bitterness and his need for revenge. "Your father hurt your mother. He nearly beat her to death, Parker. He would have gone after you, too, if Detective Roarke hadn't intervened."

Parker shook his head again. "No, no, no! I'd remember if my mother had been hurt. Don't say it again. Because I won't believe it." He pounded the fist holding the detonator against the wall.

Olivia's breath froze in her lungs and ice filled her veins. She lifted a fervent prayer to the Lord for some guidance. How could she reach this young man? How could she protect the child growing inside of her?

She wanted to live. She wanted to be a mother and to forge a future for them both. A future she wanted to share with Henry. In a moment of pure clarity, she realized she loved him. He was a man she could count on, a man she could trust with her heart. But there were obstacles in the way.

Their careers. Her investigation.

The baby. He'd already raised one teenager and had said he wasn't interest in parenting again.

The biggest obstacle at the moment, though, was Parker. If she and Riley didn't make it out of here alive, there was no future for either of them.

She had to do something to save them all. Then she could figure out what to do about her feelings for Henry.

As Parker reached for the door handle, Olivia's gaze searched wildly for something, anything, to stop him. There was a baseball sitting on the desk to her right. With two older brothers, she could throw a mean fastball and hit a target.

Parker let go of Riley to grasp the door handle. Seeing her moment, Olivia grabbed the baseball. Parker whipped around as if he sensed her movement. She threw the baseball hard, hitting Parker in the nose. She heard the delicate bones break. The kid screamed and grabbed at his face, the detonator flying from his hand, landing on the rug.

"Now!" Olivia yelled as she threw herself on the detonator.

Parker dove on top of her, clawing at her, trying to get her away from it. She heard the loud splintering of wood as the door was kicked open. The frantic barking of a dog reverberated off the walls.

Snapper latched on to Parker's leg. He screamed and rolled away from Olivia, batting at the dog biting him. "Get it off me!"

Olivia sat up, clutching the detonator to her chest. Blood from Parker's busted nose smeared her clothing.

Cody and Gavin's K-9 both sat in front of

the chair, showing their handlers the location of the explosives. From her place on the floor, Olivia had a better view of the small bundle strapped to the bottom of the desk chair with black electrical tape. A shudder worked through her at how close she'd, they'd all, come to being blown to bits.

Gavin and Lani secured Parker, putting him in handcuffs. Snapper backed off, but still growled, making it clear if he resisted the dog would attack him again.

Henry worked on the bomb strapped to the chair. Olivia held her breath, praying he didn't accidently detonate the device. His remarkably steady hands cut wires and pulled the homemade explosive apart, effectively disarming the device and saving them all.

With a shaky hand, Olivia held up the detonator. "Take this. I don't want to hold it anymore."

Gently, Henry pried the device from her fingers and laid it on the desk. He cupped her cheek for a split second before turning his attention to his sister. He undid the tape across her mouth and the zip tie holding her hands together. As soon as she was free, Riley threw her arms around her brother's neck and sobbed into his chest.

Olivia's heart throbbed with love and adrenaline. Watching the two siblings reunite made her so happy.

Then Henry was once again kneeling next to her. "Are you hurt, Olivia?"

"I'm good. It's not my blood." She wanted to hug him tight and not let go. But she had a job to do and it wasn't finished. She needed to end this debacle.

Henry helped her to her feet. Her legs wobbled with the rush of blood thrumming through her veins, though she stayed upright. She leaned on Henry for support for a moment as her equilibrium righted itself.

Before Gavin could lead Parker away, Olivia went to the young man and gripped him by the shoulders. His nose had swelled and blood dripped down his chin.

"Tell me about Davey's injuries from the incident with Detective Roarke in Owl's Head Park," Olivia demanded.

"It was all Davey's idea," Parker said. "It

was all his idea. Everything. When I told him about Detective Roarke, he planned it all. He told me what to do. He made the bombs."

"Why would Davey do this?" Olivia pressed.

Parker shrugged. "You'll have to ask him." He turned his focus on Riley. "I wouldn't have hurt you. I love you. Even if you are his sister."

Riley stared at him with anger filling her dark eyes. "You're sick. I hope I never see you again."

Parker hung his head but there were no tears, only anger twisting his face.

More police officers stormed the building. Gavin coordinated the removal of more explosives that were found in the apartment.

"I'll take care of him." Lani took Parker by the biceps. With Snapper at her side, along with several other officers, they escorted him out of the building and into a squad car.

Henry and Cody ushered Olivia and Riley out behind them. The young man would be

348 Explosive Situation

arrested and put in jail, but Olivia hoped that he would get the help he needed. In fact, she decided she would make sure he was paired with a good psychologist.

But for now, before she could look to the future, there was someone else who needed her help. Henry.

Standing on the sidewalk, she approached Gavin. "I need to speak with Davey Carrell again. Can you have him brought right away to an interrogation room at the K-9 center?"

Gavin nodded. "I'm on it."

"Lieutenant." Henry motioned for her to follow him and led her away from the crowd of officers and residents gathered to watch all the chaos. Riley and Cody were sitting in one of the K-9 unit's vehicles. "There will be time for all that. But right now, I want to make sure you and—" He stopped himself and caressed her cheek. "I want to make sure everything is okay. You mean the world to me."

It wasn't a declaration of love. They weren't free to explore this thing arcing between them. But they would be soon. She would make sure of it. "We need to get out of here. Get your sister home." She started them walking back to the car. "And I have unfinished business with Davey Carrell."

It took a couple hours for officers to bring in Davey Carrell. During that time, Olivia managed to clean up and now sat alone in an interrogation room, writing up her report while she waited. There were just a few things she needed clarified before she could take her report to the review board. She was going to recommend dismissing the charges brought against Henry.

She was confident the board would come to the same conclusion she had. Henry was a good man, full of honor and integrity, who had done his job well. Whatever injuries Davey had sustained during the altercation were not excessive. She believed Henry, not the kid who had helped terrorize the city. Thankfully no one knew of her and Henry's attraction to one another, because if it came to light, the facts of the case wouldn't matter. It would become about them.

There was a knock on the open interrogation room door. She looked up to find Eden Chang standing there. Her long dark hair was pulled back in a braid that hung over her shoulder. She wore a collared navy shirt with the K-9 unit logo and khaki pants. Her gaze was warm as she said, "Lieutenant Vance, I found something on social media I think you'll want to see."

Gathering her papers, Olivia followed Eden back to her office.

Rounding her desk, Eden said, "I told Henry, but we didn't get a chance to connect earlier. Understandable, considering." Eden sat down and fired up her monitors. "So I started trolling all the social media sites that I could find for the night of March twenty-third and decided to keep looking for any mention of the park over the past few months."

She brought up a social media account. "This was posted about two weeks ago. The poster had been visiting the city for the Fourth of July and had no idea he had evidence we needed."

She pushed Play. The skate park came into view. The setting sun cast rays over the skaters gathered around the cement ramps.

"Oh man, this dude's gonna try it," said an unseen male voice, apparently the social media account holder.

Olivia drew closer to the monitor. The "dude" in question stood at the top of what looked like a drained swimming pool, his skateboard poised over the lip of the concrete wall. He had on a helmet but there was no mistaking the face. "That's Davey Carrell."

"Yes," Eden said. "Watch what he does."

Olivia held her breath. Throughout the skate park there were ramps and various other objects for the skaters to roller up and over. But what had Olivia's attention at the bottom of the scooped bowl was a makeshift wooden ramp with large boxes placed in a row.

Davey was going to try to jump over the obstacle, Evel Knievel–style. Only on a skateboard, not a motorcycle.

Davey tapped his helmet and crouched,

with one hand on the tip of his skateboard. Then he pushed off and skated down into the bowl, up over the ramp and across the obstacle. But he lost his board midjump. For a moment, he appeared to float in the air, then he plummeted to the ground, putting out his left hand and landing hard. He let out a scream, "Ow, my wrist!" Clutching his injured limb, he rolled out of view.

"That's how he broke his wrist." Elated by this bit of evidence, Olivia pumped her fist in the air. "Can you make me a copy and send it to my email?"

Eden grinned. "I thought this might be a game changer."

"It certainly is. Did you find anything showing the confrontation between Henry and Davey?"

"As a matter of fact..." Eden's fingers flew over the keyboard again. "Same social media account. It's just the tail end of the confrontation. Like the guy had been watching the skateboarders when he turned around and realized what was happening behind him was more fascinating and started filming."

The video definitely showed Henry securing his weapon by jamming his elbow into the side of Davey's neck, then prying away his service weapon from Davey's right hand.

"Well, that clinches it." Olivia rubbed her hands together. She had the proof necessary to exonerate Henry. "I wish we'd found these sooner."

Eden shrugged. "Like I said, both of these clips were uploaded recently. Even if I had searched at the time, I wouldn't have found them."

"I'm really glad you did, Eden. You did good work. You are a real asset to the department."

Eden grinned. "Make sure you tell the sarge that."

Olivia grinned back. "Believe me, I will."

By the time she got back to the interrogation room, Davey Carrell, wearing a cast on his left wrist and a neck brace, sat between his lawyer and his parents at the metal table.

"You asked us here," the lawyer said. "What is it?"

She sat down across from the boy and ignored the lawyer. "This is your last chance to come clean, Davey. I need you to tell me the truth about what happened on the night of March twenty-third of this year at Owl's Head Park's skate park."

The boy copped an attitude, his chin jutting out. "I've already told you what happened. That pig cop broke my wrist and injured my neck."

Olivia removed her phone from the pocket of her gray suit jacket, opened her email and found the video of Davey skating. She turned the phone so that all four people on the other side of the table could view the screen.

"What is this?" the lawyer asked.

"Watch." Olivia pushed Play.

When the video ended. Davey was sitting back in his seat, looking a little sick.

"Are you really going to stick with your story?" Olivia asked.

"Objection," the lawyer said. "We were

not given that video to review and it doesn't show anything relevant."

Flicking a glance at the well-dressed, no doubt highly paid attorney, Olivia said, "This isn't a court of law, Counselor. And I was just apprised of this video." She found the next email sent by Eden. "As well as this one." She played the video of Henry securing his weapon.

"Davey," Mr. Carrell intoned with disgust. "You lied."

With a mulish expression on his face, Davey's shoulders slumped.

"Parker says you were the mastermind," Olivia stated, gauging the kid's reaction.

"No way!" Davey sat up, outrage making his face red. "It was all him. Parker spotted that cop when he came into the place where Parker works. He concocted the whole thing."

Olivia narrowed her gaze on the young man. "You didn't help him build the bombs?"

"Not even. That's beyond me," Davey said, sitting back. "Parker is wicked smart.

And he can be scary at times. You wouldn't want to cross him."

Not sure how to feel about Davey's assessment of Parker, she kept her focus on the matter she needed resolved. "Then you admit that Detective Roarke did not break your wrist and that you tried to relieve him of his sidearm?"

"Don't answer that," the lawyer interjected.

Davey shrugged. "They got the video, man. I never wanted to do this whole thing, but Parker talked me into it."

Beside him his mother made a noise of distress.

Davey glanced at her then turned back to Olivia. "Yes, I broke my wrist on that stupid fall." Davey touched the brace around his neck "But he did hurt my neck when…" He grimaced and slumped again. "He did hurt my neck."

"What about the vandalism to Detective Roarke's vehicle?" Olivia asked. "Were you involved in that?"

Davey shook his head. "I haven't been allowed to leave the house for months."

Satisfied, Olivia gathered her papers and slipped her phone back into her pocket. "Counselor, I assume you'll recant the charges against Detective Roarke."

"In light of this new information, yes, we will ask the DA to drop the charges."

"Good," Olivia said. "I'm sure the DA will be in contact in regard to charging Davey with a felony for attempting to disarm Detective Roarke."

The lawyer rose and faced the family. "You'll need to find new representation. I'll send you my bill." He walked out the door.

As the Carrells left, Olivia shook her head.

Now that the case against Henry would be dismissed, she was free to decide her future. She pressed her hand to her belly.

Something had become clear to her these past few days. Despite her desire to make her family proud by staying in the family tradition of law enforcement and first responders, she wanted something different in life. She wanted to help people in a different way. She was going to resign from the force.

If someone had taken an interest in Parker all those years ago, maybe he would have been mentally stable and lived his life making better choices.

She planned to use her degree in psychology and criminal justice to offer support and assistance to trauma victims like Parker before it ever became too late.

Henry stood on the grass outside the training center and the K-9 unit building with Cody, the puppies and Brooke, the mama dog. He'd been pacing inside when the vet, Gina, had asked him to make himself useful by taking the dogs out for a break.

Cody and Brooke were keeping the puppies in line while Henry continued his pacing. He'd seen Davey and his entourage leave the headquarters building several minutes ago.

It took all of Henry's willpower not to go find Olivia and ask her what had happened. Was she filing her report now? What was she recommending? Would he resume his duties? Or be charged with excessive force?

He refrained from seeking her out because it wouldn't be appropriate. Though he wanted to know her conclusions, he told himself to exercise some patience. He would find out in due time.

But his career hung in the balance.

His life hung in the balance.

A life he wanted to share with Olivia and her child. He hadn't foreseen falling hard for the beautiful and caring woman. Finding romance while embroiled in an internal affairs investigation had thrown his carefully planned life into chaos. A good kind of chaos. The kind that made his heart pound with joy and terror all at once.

Yet, how could they ever be together while their jobs kept them at odds?

He searched his heart and realized he'd willingly give up the force if it meant he could spend his life with the woman he'd come to love.

"Are you puppy-sitting?"

He whirled around and found Olivia walking toward him. She was so beautiful, so regal, dressed in a gray suit with a pale purple blouse. Her amber eyes sparkled and the smile on her face caused a ripple of joy to cascade through him. She was warm and alive and glowing.

She held out her hand. Without second-guessing himself, he grasped her smaller hand within his, loving the feel of her soft skin pressed again his palm. Glancing around to make sure no one was watching, he tugged her closer.

She squeezed his hand. "You're in the clear."

"What do you mean?"

"Davey has retracted his accusations. We have proof he was lying. The case will be dismissed. You're free to resume your duties with the K-9 unit."

His knees nearly buckled. But he locked them and stared into her eyes. "That's good news."

Learning he was no longer under investigation lifted a heavy weight off his mind, making him a bit light-headed. He could take a full breath and not feel the pressure of the false accusation.

Olivia squeezed his hand. "And I've decided to leave the force and open my own trauma counseling practice here in Brooklyn."

For a moment the ramifications of her announcement left him speechless. She was resigning from the NYPD. Finding his voice, he said, "Are you sure? I mean, I've already said you made a wonderful counselor, but you're also a really great investigator."

The determination and confidence in her eyes had his heart pounding.

"I am sure. It's what I want to do with my life. How I want to make a difference in the lives of others."

He so admired this remarkable woman. He swallowed, his throat suddenly closing on the words bursting to get out. If he didn't say what was in his heart now, he might never get another chance. "I have to tell you something. And I'll understand if what I'm about to say isn't wanted, but I need you to know. I've fallen in love you, Olivia. You are such a kind and caring woman. You've opened my eyes to viewing the world in different ways. I want you to know I would never purposely hurt or deceive you. I want the best for you and your child."

Olivia's eyes widened and for a fraction of a second he feared she would reject him. Then a soft, beaming smile broke out on her lovely face. "I've fallen for you, too, Henry. I know you are a man of integrity and honor. A man I can trust with my heart."

Relief swept through him. "I'm so glad to hear that."

Then worry clouded her eyes. "Henry, the baby and I come as a package deal."

"I know." He kissed her hand. "I wouldn't have it any other way. I want to be a father. From the beginning. Now that I've had a little practice, I'll be better at it the second time around."

She grinned. "Or a third?"

"Yes." He chuckled. Love and hope and elation filled his chest to overflowing. "Whatever you want. Whenever you want. With God as our rudder, we'll do just fine."

One of the puppies, Maverick, wedged himself between Olivia's legs, his little body quivering with obvious excitement.

Olivia bent down and picked up the puppy, snuggling him close. "Do you think Riley will be okay with us?"

"She's already given us her blessing," he told her. "She told me you would be a great catch."

Olivia laughed. "She told me the same thing about you."

"Then I guess we better not disappoint her." He tugged Olivia close for a kiss.

* * * * *

Look for Belle Montera's story,
Tracking a Kidnapper, *by Valerie Hansen,*
the next book in the True Blue K-9 Unit:
Brooklyn series, available in August 2020.

True Blue K-9 Unit: Brooklyn
These police officers fight
for justice with the
help of their brave canine partners.

Copycat Killer *by Laura Scott,*
April 2020
Chasing Secrets *by Heather Woodhaven,*
May 2020
Deadly Connection *by Lenora Worth,*
June 2020
Explosive Situation *by Terri Reed,*
July 2020
Tracking a Kidnapper *by Valerie Hansen,*
August 2020
Scene of the Crime *by Sharon Dunn,*
September 2020